The Smiling Assassin

Thomas Abraham

Rachel

Regards & Best wishes

Thomas
18ᵗʰ 24

Copyright © Thomas Abraham 2021

All rights reserved.

All characters in this publication are fictitious and any resemblance to real persons, living or dead, is purely coincidental.

This book is sold subject to the condition that it shall not, by way of trade or otherwise, be hired out, lent or resold, or otherwise circulated without the author's/publisher's prior consent in any form of binding or cover other than that in which it is published and without a similar condition including this condition being imposed on the subsequent publisher.

The moral rights of the author have been asserted.

Dedication

To all those who suffer from family cruelty.

Contents

1 Match Seeking 1

2 Mark – Jack of All Trades 18

3 The Wedding 23

4 Passage to England 35

5 Honeymoon 53

6 Gentleman Jim 62

7 Baby Girl 68

8 Moving Home 95

9 Marriage on the Rocks 107

10 Domestic Strife 131

11 Illness Strikes 135

12 Journey's End 146

13 Farewell 152

14 Parted Ways 166

1

Match Seeking

The phone rang three times, shuddering the solemn silence with shrills.

'I found a match for Julie,' Mark exulted in excitement and a vibrant explosion of uncontrollable joy.

Molly had just returned from church and was still in the orange and maroon silk saree, the perfect blend of modern and traditional design. The saree was for the woman who was looking for something very much different, acceptable and diverting the attention of all who happened to see her.

'Oh, that is great; tell me more.'

'Not now, I'll keep you in suspense for the time being. You will like him.'

There was a short pause. She was caught in a cobweb of mystery and suspense.

'OK, thanks.' She sighed with an infused infatuation. Molly was a highly demanding and materialistic lady whose policy in life was simple - 'I come in the middle, I come last and I come first.' She was a person who believed that there was a correlation between the social status and the human worth. She always felt superiority over those from lower social classes, education levels or other social areas. Most of the time she was standoffish, stubborn, snobbish, and stern. The fundamental values of a 'lady' were a bit of an antiquity to her. She had a very picky lifestyle. She felt she was always right. If somebody criticized her, she would be fiercely defensive and create a scene. Her interactions reminded one of Chaucer, a poet moving in the court circles who noted the provincial French spoken by the Prioress among the Canterbury pilgrims:

And French she spoke full fair and fetisly
After the school of Stratford atte Bowe,
For French of Paris was to her unknowe

Molly went to the kitchen to put the kettle on, nipped to the loo and went to the bedroom to get changed. The saree was carefully folded into a palisade and hung at the far corner of the wardrobe where she had a collection of expensive sarees to suit every occasion. When she opened it, she got a feeling that she had nothing to wear. She got changed into a satin soft full slip silk sleepwear negligee nightgown and went back to the kitchen. There was a sudden gush of cold breeze when the cat flap was thrust open. The cat, Jerome, breezed in with a gift, a mouse. He left the hapless half-dead creature on the floor. It started wriggling away sluggishly but Jerome was play-chasing the victim like a toddler playing with a toy. As a routine, Molly always made sure that she was at the centre of various acts of charity and piety in the community.

Molly was in a trance. She could not wait. Although she picked up the phone and pressed the redial button to ring Mark, she paused with self-induced control, hesitated, and did not complete the call. She made her favourite drink, mixing up Cointreau, dry gin and lemon juice, the *White Lady Cocktail,* sat down on the settee and sipped it slowly and surely enjoying every sip all the way through. She was dark in complexion and less than five feet tall. But with six inches high heels, heavy make-up and the constant company of white ladies, she always felt she was one among them. She considered herself well above her country mates from Sri Lanka, who were mainly shopkeepers. Although she could speak Sinhala, she felt it was below her standard to use it and always conversed only in English. She always preferred to dance only to her own music. She was uncertain and unpunctual in daily life and used to boast that Hollywood actress Elizabeth Taylor was always late for her assignments. Her basic philosophy in life was that she would become friendly with people who could be alluded to her advantages.

If she noticed a new wrinkle or new strand of grey hair, she would keep worrying about it until she could conceal it. Her bathroom looked more like a hair salon with an assortment of hair dyes and cosmetics. She meticulously dyed her hair blond golden. At close range, the wrinkles on her face looked like an interconnected tessellating network of mud cracks on the sun-scorched plains of Africa. They were carefully concealed by concentrated layers of foundation and creams. Her nickname was 'cake face' since many times her make-up was overshadowing and overpowering the occasions.

She was a prominent activist in the church. Her main duties involved conducting the daily matins, publishing the banns of marriage, distributing Holy Communion and assisting the priest in pastoral matters. She used to preen, crow and gloat of her work and made a spectacle of herself. She was a regular fixture at the church charity functions making donations, insisted on photographs and made every effort to list them in the parish bulletins. Her poise and posture were patronizing and parading of her feats. Being possessed by passion and pride, she always sprayed herself with Jo Malone Grapefruit Cologne since she was told by a friend that when women sprayed themselves with the scent of grapefruit, they were perceived by men to be seven years younger. It had an uplifting scent and wearing that turned the heads of others in the vicinity. She would always put on a smile and loved to live in dream, not just one but in so many new dreams. Her other moniker was Hyacinth of *Keeping up Appearances*. Her feisty personality flitted between frivolous and serious matters. Even in subjects which she had no knowledge, Molly used to be opinionated, challenging and disruptive in discussions. She used to indulge in a diatribe of bilge in most matters.

The parish priest, Fr Thomas, was an Irishman, just over fifty-five, tall, staid, respectable and rather heavy with a beard which was as thick as a gardening broom with bristles sticking out in all directions. The streaks of grey on the beard gave the impression that he had just returned after a walk on a frosty winter day. On close inspection, the curls of hair looked like moss. There were spider-leg wrinkles at the outer angles of his eyes which danced around while giving animated sermons. Molly used to invite Fr Thomas every month for a delicious Sri-Lankan meal. On the Father's 55th birthday celebration, she quoted St John Vianney, the patron saint of priests. 'The priest will not understand the greatness of his office until he is in heaven. If he understood it on earth, he would die not of fear.'

***

Mark was in Sri Lanka for two weeks. He had been running helter-skelter with a sole and singular aim - to find a nice boy for Julie, his daughter. He had advertised in the *Colombo Echo* for a suitable match. He had seen three boys already. The fourth one struck him straightaway. Jacob, a solicitor by trade, smart-looking, 5 ft 9 inches tall, lanky with a beaming smile. He had completed a law degree two years back. Mark thought he could bring him over to England soon and get him a decent job. Also, the dowry was not big. He could retire in five years' time and move to Porto. Mark had a patent megawatt smile, poise and intelligence which were his arms to win over people who came across him. He was a man with a bonanza of riches.

He recollected the happy memories of Porto while holidaying there. Porto is a coastal city in northwest Portugal known for its stately bridges and port wine production. Its narrow cobbled streets wind past merchants' houses and cafes. The São Francisco Church is known for its lavish baroque interior with ornate gilded carvings. The palatial 19th century *Palácio de Bolsa,* formerly a stock market, was built to impress potential European investors.

'Sir, we have reached the hotel,' the taxi driver reminded him politely. After giving him money for lunch, Mark said,

'I am going to have a lie down, so I won't be going anywhere today.' He went to the room, which was on the fifth floor. He drew the curtains and shook his head in tranquil exasperation. What a lovely view! The deep blue Indian Ocean majestically waving at him, the shimmering beams of sunlight reflecting on the white sand giving an appearance of pearls, the seagulls fiercely doing an acrobatic fly past competing for their lunch. The seagull represented adaptability and resourcefulness, as well as opportunities and favourable circumstances. It meant focussing on the need to find ways to survive and doing even the uncomfortable just to succeed. He took inspiration from the birds.

He got changed, lay on the bed, and pressed the calling bell. The waiter appeared soon.

'Can you get me a double Dalwhinnie whisky?'

'Yes, Sir; anything to eat?'

'Get me some pappad, lime pickle and a fish fry now.'

In ten minutes, the trolley entered steered by the waiter, carefully and respectfully, with an infectious and intriguing smile. He poured the whisky from the bottle into the glass. Mark looked, smelt and had a sip in a carefully choreographed fashion. While enjoying his favourite drink, the prying eyes of the waiter raised his curiosity.

The waiter said, 'This is awfully expensive; do you always drink this whisky?'

'Yes, money is no problem for me. This is the best I like. I used to work in Edinburgh, not far from where this whisky is made. Dalwhinnie is the name of the place where it is distilled. The smell is of medium-sweet sherry, sultanas and of sweet smoke. It's smooth on the palate, with a subtle note of peat.' Mark gave a dogmatic description of the whisky; the waiter stood pale and immovable with mouth half-open and staring with a wide gaze in a state of amazement with a laboured effort of attention.

'Can you bring a chicken biriyani in half an hour?'

'Yes, Sir.' The waiter paused and glanced at Mark. The message was clear. Mark gave him a crisp 20 rupees note. 'Thank you, Sir.' The waiter made a brisk exit and gleefully checked the tip he had received that day, 270 rupees. He pondered, 'A very good day in office.'

Shortly after, Mark had the lunch and slipped into a state of slumber. He had already taken photos and videos of Jacob and family. Jacob's father had given a family album, ready for dispatch like a car dealer's doctored brochure about his car. The mission was halfway through. Anyway, Mark had made up his mind. Now, all he needs to do is convince Julie that this is an ideal match. Although the flight was next week, Mark decided to get back to England as soon as possible. He went to the Emirates office. The sales clerk said that there was a flight next day but he would have to pay £75 extra for changing the schedule. He pulled out his credit card in a hurry and paid out post-haste.

The taxi driver was waiting. When he was told of the change of plan, the driver Raj was a bit despondent. He said, 'Sir, you had booked the taxi for three weeks; Now, I will lose a week's job since I had turned down other bookings.'

Mark thought he was right in his stand. He said, 'Ok; we will sort something out. Let us have lunch. Take me to the best five-star hotel of your choice.'

They arrived at Hotel Sealord. Mark planned a hidden diplomatic move; invited Raj to join him for the meal. Raj could not believe his luck. The gala dinner was the first one Raj has seen in his life because it was sumptuous, of five-star quality and most importantly complimentary. He seized the moment with both hands. It started with Moët & Chandon champagne served in a flute. Raj kept gazing at the flute with an air of awe and admiration. It tasted of a combined delicacy, subtle freshness, and skilful blending.

While tasting, Mark commented, 'It has more grace, finesse and lightness than traditional champagnes with fine balance between nose and palate.' For Raj, it was a novelty and he felt Mark was using too technical terms which he could not fathom out. Their starter was smoked salmon with brown bread and butter.

Mark quipped, 'Scotland has the best salmon in the world. There they say that the rivers run true and sweet.' Russian salad composed of carrots, beetroots, potatoes, and peas give a colourful display on the table. Raj's salivary system went into overdrive. The main dish was beef stroganov. Mark went on, 'This recipe was created by Russian General Stroganov, who served Ivan the Great.' Roast potatoes and fried rice were available to choose from. Aubergine moussaka and French beans in tomato sauce were side dishes. Semolina and wine pudding rounded off the sumptuous dinner. He was so tired after the heaviest meal of his life, he felt like a python who had eaten a heavy prey.

Returning to the hotel, Mark told him, 'Shall we meet halfway? I will pay you two days taxi rent extra as a compromise.'

Raj nodded in approval. 'Thank you, Sir. I hope you will let me know in advance when you are coming back for the wedding. I will do a discount for you.' He said it all in a hurry to grab the business. Both parties were happy.

The next day, Raj dropped Mark at the airport. As the last act of kindness, Mark gave Raj a Marks & Spencer shirt which he had as a spare. Raj was well pleased!

The flight was on time and uneventful. Mark landed in Manchester. The pick-up taxi was waiting. He reached home, Halifax, in forty minutes.

Their house was in Sowerby Bridge, five miles from Halifax town centre. It was called *'Majully'* encompassing names of Mark, Julie and Molly. The town was originally a fording point over the once much wider River Calder where it joined the River Ryburn. The town takes its name from the historic bridge which spans the river in the town centre. Textiles and engineering industries grew up around the bridge. By the mid-19th century the population had grown and the settlement became an urban district in the West Riding of Yorkshire in 1894.

The detached two-storey house was situated on the top of the hill with an acre of land and beautifully set front and back gardens. The winding road going into the property was met with two catalpa trees which stood as tall as sentry guards. They had white, showy flowers, giant heart-shaped leaves, dangling bean-like seed pods and twisting trunks and branches. There were four double bedrooms with fitted wardrobes and en-suites, two reception rooms, a spacious kitchen, utility room and cloak room. The décor was traditional with an original fireplace and coving.

The back garden was weed-free, filled with vigorous plants and interspersed wide wood-chipped walkways. Flowers and herbs graced the garden. Julie had skilfully grown lettuces in different shades, onions, and spinach.

There were trees near the boundaries. The silver maple tree produced a lovely shimmery effect due to the silvery undersides of its leaves. American sweetgum with its star-shaped leaves, compact crown fruit, and twigs with unique corky growths called wings stood out since the glossy green leaves turned into shades of yellow, orange, red and purple in the autumn. The Weeping Willow displayed an open crown of wispy, ground-sweeping branches and long, slender leaves. Its yellow twigs and green foliage were heart-warming and soothing.

The fruit trees were Mark's passion. The Red Jonathan apple trees produced beautiful, bright red apples which were crisp and juicy. They were good for eating fresh, freezing and cooking. The European pear tree produced large, smooth, shiny, round yellow fruits with a red cheek, thick skin, and flesh that was juicy and creamy with a mild flavour. It bloomed with white flowers. The belle of Georgia peach produced brilliant red flowers each spring and large fruits. The peaches were very firm and highly flavoured, with creamy white freestone flesh tinged with red. The cherry tree produced large, heart-shaped fruits with a firm, meaty, purplish-red flesh and a semi-free stone.

There was a well-fenced duck pond with two resident white-faced whistling ducks whose quacks quivered constantly in the garden. At times, they would hiss and grunt. They always acted as if they were the sole owners of the pond.

Mark had a one-to-one discussion with Julie and showed her the photographs of Jacob and family. Julie carefully went through all and said,

'I don't mind looking at all these; but it is my life. I would like all of us to go and see him for myself before making a decision.' Mark thought she was right, and she had every right to say so.

Three days later, Mark took Molly out for a meal to discuss the plans. They took the joint decision to get a professional photographer to do a home video. Although he had shown Jacob and family the photos of Julie, Mark got her approval for an up-to-date video. Molly was in full agreement since that would also give her an opportunity to broadcast her glittering beauty, silk saree, gold ornaments, Omega watch and all the associated paraphernalia.

Julie was a natural beauty with a pale complexion, stunning figure, and a flowing elegance in every movement. There was a girlish look of innocence which was manifest. The make-up artist, Nicole, had never seen a lady so intimately revealed and ungroomed. She felt that Julie was a typical virgin in body, mind, and spirit. She kept chatting non-stop to make Julie more relaxed while carrying on with her mundane tasks.

She said to Julie, 'If God had created more people like you, I would have been jobless.'

'Why?'

'Because you were born beautiful; you don't really need much make-up.'

Flattery had its effect. Julie started talking and giggling with a sense of fervour, excitement, and the anticipation of impressing her potential future spouse. Nicole was in sole charge of transforming the shy girl into a potential bride-to-be. She scanned the wall clock; she had two hours to complete the task. She started with the hair, transforming from black to dark purple, to blonde and lavender pink, like an artist creating such magic. She paired the colour with luscious long locks crafted into giant and bouncy curls. She trimmed and shaded the eyebrows and applied facial cleanser, scrubbed, and moisturized. Then she applied primer, foundation and produced stoned rose cheeks. When finished, Nicole not only just highlighted the existing features but also created a new image.

Julie's jewellery collection was opened to pick and choose. Nicole chose a Stellato amethyst and diamond heart necklace in white gold. This was romantic and luxurious displaying a sparkling violet amethyst gemstone carved into a heart shape and encircled by a halo of shimmering diamonds. The white gold setting completed a high-quality look. Matching sapphire and diamond belle drop earrings in white gold were put on.

There was a million-dollar question; to wear a saree or not? Nicole suggested that this was a home video, and it was better not to get too overdressed. Julie also felt the same. Nicole suggested she wear the *cheongsam*, a body-hugging dress which would spell out her distinctive elegant figure and popularly worn by upper-class women in Asia. Among the dozen pairs of shoes, Nicole selected a stunning court shoe in sumptuous suede - Moda In Pelle Ilari Fuschia Suede - with an elegant, pointed toe, set on a gorgeous metal filigree heel with entwined floral metalwork and gemstone detailing.

The photographer Edwin came bang on time. It was a sunny day with a light breeze. He gave an outline of the task - just be as normal as possible, walk around the house chatting, then take some staged photographs inside and then outside in the garden. It all went according to plan. The photographs and video were sent to Jacob's family.

Seeing those, Jacob's mother Lilly commented, 'She looks

like a Bollywood star.' Jacob was overwhelmed and eager to see the real person. He started dreaming. In the night he scanned through the photos of various Bollywood stars.

Two weeks later, Mark and his family flew to Colombo. They chose to stay in Hotel Sealord and got Raj's taxi. Raj gave a vivid running commentary of ferrying many people settled abroad, whose wedding-related transport he had undertaken in the past. Jacob's dad, Pinto, invited them for dinner next day. It was a lavish affair. After the customary greetings and introduction, they separated into pairs - Mark and Pinto retired into the bar adjacent to the kitchen, Molly and Lilly sat in the kitchen and Julie was left alone in the lounge already set up with light music in the background. Lilly was a caring, compassionate, and considerate woman with a great sense of humour. Jacob was outside overseeing the gardener.

Pinto had a selection of whiskies on show and invited Mark to make the choice. He chose Royal Salute, a unique style of the blend, which was manifest in the luscious, round and rewardingly warm format with aromas of sweet plums, marzipan and vanilla. Lilly specially made Paradise Cocktail, which was composed of apricot brandy, dry gin and orange juice, and both enjoyed it. Facts, fiction, and gossip all went up in the air interspersed with intertwining diffused curls of smoke from Pinto's pipe producing a misty whirlwind. All were blowing their own trumpets except Julie, who kept a low dignified profile. Julie was immersed in thought about meeting the man in person. Although they both had seen photographs of each other, the sense of immense anticipation filled her heart with a flutter. She started sweating due to sheer excitement. In a few moments, the reality would dawn upon her. She couldn't wait. She was carefully escorted by Lilly into a mini reception room, which had been meticulously transformed into a stylish art gallery featuring wall-mounted photographs of Jacob from childhood, the school tennis champion receiving a trophy, making speech at a college union meeting, meeting the local mayor as a scout etc. *Looks impressive; a boy of many talents indeed.* Julie's imagination went amok.

The door was gently opened by Lilly and Julie breezed in like a fairy in a carefully choreographed style. Jacob got up from the settee and with a beaming smile, greeted Julie and offered a chair to sit down. They both felt an aura of strangeness and eagerness which had never been experienced, heard, or seen in the past. Julie was wearing Eternity by Calvin Klein which was packed with romantic notes of freesia, lily of the valley and spicy carnation causing Jacob's head to fall over heels.

Julie felt his gaze on her face which slowly descended on her firm high breasts and stayed there emanating warmth. *Don't stare at me,* she felt like telling him but curbed as the thought flashed in her head. A sense of discrete innate sensual pleasure started bubbling and frothing like foam in her blood. She sat leaning forward as if caught in a magnetic field. She paused, expecting him to talk. Both of them felt lost in a trance of timelessness like being engulfed in a space capsule. They didn't know how long it took before they started talking.

Anyway, the eyes had met; messages were exchanged, and the minds were read mutually in Morse code. Jacob felt that it was a man's job to break the ice, to talk first in this situation. His throat was dry, and stomach was cart-wheeling. Outside, the sun goddess was smiling, and a gentle breeze caressed the coconut tree leaves rhythmically symbolizing a welcome dance. He said, 'Oh, it is nice and sunny.'

'Ya, it looks like a nice day.'

Peering out through the window, Julie pointed to the nearby mango tree on which a lily of the valley had entwined itself and remarked, 'How sweet the scent of its pendent bell-shaped white flowers is, which are borne in sprays in spring.'

Both felt they have managed to break the silence.

'What would you like to drink?'

'A glass of red wine please.'

Jacob thought he should seize this mini chance to impress. He did not know much about wine. Masquerading his ignorance in this area, he just got up and like a guided missile went to the minibar. He took three bottles - Chateau Pontet-Canet, Chateau La Conseillante and Chambolle-Musigny and marched first but then deliberately slowed down his pace to reach Julie.

'Wow,' Julie sighed.

Julie couldn't make up which one to choose but went for Chambolle-Musigny. Jacob carefully poured it into the glass. Jacob went back to get a glass of white wine and they both stood up and raised their glasses, said 'Cheers' and started sipping.

From the way Jacob handled the wine glasses, Julie could easily make out that he was a novice to drinking. Julie tactically recalled her A-level project and started giving a masterclass on wine drinking.

She said, 'Cheers is simply a symbolic and succinct way of toasting with the wish of good cheer and good health to those around us, an exercise of camaraderie. Clinking glasses with others before a drink is a custom that has been practiced for centuries.'

Jacob inquisitively peered into her eyes with a fervent smile. 'It is believed that clinking glasses was done during toasts, because *sound* helped to incite all five senses, completing the drinking experience. Drinking was also a coming together of friends, so by physically touching glasses, drinkers become part of a community in celebration.'

'In medieval times, glasses were clinked, and people cheered loudly to ward off any evil spirits. It was also thought that you would clink glasses to spill some on the floor, leaving some for the bad spirits in hopes that they would leave you alone. A German tradition was to bang mugs of alcohol on the table and yell loudly to scare away ghosts or evil spirits. Back in the days when poisoning a foe's drink was a convenient way to murder him, it was believed that if glasses were filled to the brim and then clinked hard, a bit of alcohol from each glass would spill into the other. Mixing drinks and then taking a sip was a gesture that the drinks were unharmed.

'Toasting is thought to come from a libation of a sacred liquid offered to the gods in exchange for a wish or a prayer for health. It was Greek and Roman tradition to leave an offering to the gods during celebrations. In Greek mythology, the god of wine, Bacchus, was often toasted. Today, we still raise our glasses upwards to the heavens as if offering to the gods a toast to the health of the living.'

Jacob sat listening with his mouth half-open and an admiring, faint and fading smile at Julie. He was astonished at her knowledge.

The game kicked off in style, Julie had scored the first goal. Now, it was Jacob's time. Jacob pondered what to start with. He did not have to think much. *I will go for law.*

He started. 'While I was at college, I noted lots of unjust things around me in the society. That is why I wanted to take up law.'

Julie looked straight into his eyes and with a radiant smile, listened carefully giving him the much-needed attention he deserved.

'Legal history is closely connected to the development of civilizations and is set in the wider context of social history. The origin of Lady Justice was Justitia, the Goddess of Justice within

Roman mythology, introduced by the Emperor Augustus. The Temple of Justitia was established in Rome in 13BC by the Emperor Tiberius. Lady Justice was most often depicted with a set of scales typically suspended from one hand measuring the strengths of a case's support and opposition. Justitia was only commonly represented as 'blind' since justice must be meted out impartially. The sword represented authority in ancient times and conveys the idea that justice can be swift and final.

Julie's face said it all. She appeared dazed like a minuet of the misunderstood. Jacob ardently admired her movements even to the nanosecond.

Final score- scores level or Julie slightly ahead by one point? Now, it is crunch time, the *happy minute* of the meeting. The million-dollar question was how to find out whether the matchmaking experiment has worked? What is the acid test?

Neither Julie nor Jacob dared to throw the question on the face 'Do you like me?'.

Bang on time, Lilly and Molly strolled in and invited them to join for dinner. Since all were intoxicated, they ate in a ravenous and noisy manner. There was a brief secret conclave of the quartet of the senior citizens after dinner. All were keen to find out the outcome - do they like each other? They concluded that it was the ladies' job to find out. After about an hour and half, they had a very heavy meal and returned to the hotel by eleven at night.

Next morning, when Jacob returned from his daily walk, Lilly asked him in casual way, 'What do you think of Julie? Do you like her?'

Jacob paused, smiled, and peered into her eyes and sighed. His voice quaked, 'Yes, Mom.'

'Is it a definite yes?'

He nodded twice with a broad smile and seal of approval.

Delicate diplomatic manoeuvres were being undertaken at the hotel room. Mark and Molly though it was better to bring the topic towards the end of dinner. While they were having post-dinner coffee, Mark went to the toilet after gesturing Molly. She leaned forward, held Julie's hand and asked her in the meekest and sweetest note,

'Do you like Jacob?'

Julie put on a deliberate pause and murmured with the pair of flashing eyes and responded, 'Ya, he seems like a nice bloke.'

Mark returned. He could read the outcome explicitly by the body language. He wanted to confirm. 'Is everything OK? Shall we go ahead?'

Both Julie and Molly nodded approvingly.

Next day, Pinto rang Mark. Everybody was happy. The wedding was fixed to take place four weeks later in Colombo.

2

Mark – Jack of All Trades

Mark was the son of affluent parents in Colombo. He was pampered, being the only offspring, right from childhood. He was never short of toys, expensive clothes, and luxury trips. His father was a politician who was always travelling away for work-related matters and other burning issues which could be capitalized in politics. Mother was a simple housewife with extremely limited contact with the outside world.

When Mark was 10 years old, he was punched by two of his classmates after a football match. His father being a big shot, took matters in his own hands and administered instant justice. He went to the boys' houses, confronted the parents head-on and threatened to retaliate in style if anything similar happened in future. Also, by complaining to the headmaster, the kids got a nasty telling off at school. They were made to apologize publicly in assembly. After all, politics was a power game. Most people feared politicians in general.

After passing his matriculate examination, Mark's father liaised with his cousin who was already a US citizen and decided to send him to California for his university education. Thus, Mark ended up as a lodger-relative. Mark settled smoothly into university life. He started going out with friends, and the neon-lit life slowly attracted his attention and life became very colourful. When he was 23, Mark met a lady from his junior batch in the law college. She was 22, petite, called Jessica and hailed from the Philippines. They started going out and soon ended up in a full-blown romance. Mark was never short of money. He made sure that he always appeared in public in smart and expensive dress, a Rolex watch and Cerruti fragrance. Things got out of hand in six months, however. Jessica got pregnant. Mark was caught up in a dilemma. He was frozen and frenzied with fear, resulting in a state of self-induced isolation. He had nobody to talk this matter through with. He could not discuss this with his uncle or his parents. Jessica was in no mood to let him go free. She knew he was rich. She started making demands for cash on a weekly basis.

After about a few months, cashflow started slowing down. Mark had an open cheque arrangement his dad made with his uncle; he could borrow cash as needed. So, Mark started borrowing from uncle. Uncle grew suspicious. One day, the cleaner lady found a letter partially open lying in the wedge between the mattress and valance, which she gave to Mark's auntie. It was a bombshell. The letter was three-and-a-half pages long, professionally written without any corrections, and in a loving but serious tone. The crux of the demand was Mark had to marry her soon at the register office officially; otherwise, she would go public. Uncle rang Mark's dad. He really went into a state of disbelief and disarray. If it were in Sri Lanka, he would have handled and settled it as he wished.

Being the only son, the decision was to go along with Mark's wish and to support him. Mark was drawn into a deeper hole. He had no choice. They got married soon with two of his batch mates as witnesses. Mark's dad did not want any publicity. Jessica gave birth to a baby boy. She continued to stay with her parents who had been in America for 30 years. Mark took his Law Degree and wanted to return to Colombo since his dad got him a job in a top legal firm. Jessica did not want to move to Sri

Lanka. The tug of war went on for about two months. Her parents were very protective of her and she was always leaning onto them for advice. The parents forced her to divorce Mark. She went along. Mark left America as a divorced man. The bond with Jessica ended abruptly. A sordid chapter closed. Mark flew back to Colombo. There was no contact after that.

Mark loved music and tennis right from an early age. He had a charming, cerebral and consuming passion for tennis. His effervescent enthusiasm led to him going to watch many international matches. While waiting to explore further options, Mark was deeply touched with the news of drought and famine in Ghana. He volunteered to work in Ghana on a charity mission. He had always been a benevolent man. Action Aid was an international charity that worked with women and girls living in poverty. The dedicated staff were changing the world with motivated women and girls. They were trying to fight to end violence and wipe out poverty so that all women everywhere could create the future they wanted. The vision was a just, equitable and sustainable world in which every person enjoyed the right to a life of dignity, freedom from poverty and all forms of oppression.

The approach involved building relationships with communities, especially women and girls who were often the most affected by poverty and discrimination. Each team of combat squads was made up of a cross section of the community and were actively engaged in those communities by presenting talks at schools, identifying issues, and working with the police to bring perpetrators to justice.

Action Aid provided seed banks for useful crops to those in need to ensure food security. In many parts of the world where crops have failed due to rising temperatures and erratic rainfall, the charity worked closely with the agricultural communities to provide them with climate-resilient crop seeds so families could eat and maintain a livelihood.

After working in Ghana for three months, Jack was called back home. After brief formalities, in a few weeks, his wedding with Molly took place. Then, life took a different direction. He had to be a breadwinner. His dad was very influential with wide contacts in the higher circles of society. It did not take long. Jack got a trainee job in a legal firm in Edinburgh.

He flew into Edinburgh, Scotland's compact and hilly capital. It has a medieval Old Town and an elegant Georgian New Town with gardens and neoclassical buildings. Looming over the city was Edinburgh Castle, home to Scotland's crown jewels and the Stone of Destiny, used in the coronation of Scottish rulers. Arthur's Seat is an imposing peak in Holyrood Park with sweeping views, and Calton Hill was topped with monuments and memorials.

Jack enjoyed the job and got on well within the firm. In three months, there was a fresh opportunity. One of the partners in the firm developed a stroke and decided to take early retirement. Mark was soon drafted in to take his role. He seized the opportunity with both hands and worked hard to prove his mettle. The firm liked his input and after a trial period of three months, he was enrolled as a full-time partner in the firm. He brought Molly to join him.

Being a solicitor, Mark moved with the upper echelons of the society which he and Molly enjoyed very much. The class culture had been shown to have a strong influence on the mundane lives of people, affecting everything from the way they maintained romantic relationships and the dress they wore to their type of dwellings. Because the social networks tended to be within their own class, they acculturated to and learned the values and behaviours of their own class. The impact of class culture on delineating a social hierarchy was significant. Mark slowly turned into a cavalier maverick with his own trademark wince and witticism. His intensity in getting things done was impressive.

He had an infectious sense of adventure as well as a mischievous sense of humour. Armed with sharp wit, he would hold the attention of any room due to his charm. People never knew what he might say next. His enduring influence and presence of mind helped to develop Julie into a mature lady.

Molly got pregnant. Unfortunately, after seven weeks she suffered a miscarriage. After eighteen months, she got pregnant again and gave birth to Julie.

Mark had various friends spread all over the UK. One of his batch mates from law school in Colombo was an established barrister in Manchester. They used to exchange visits fairly frequently. By coincidence, a single-handed solicitor in Halifax suddenly died and an opportunity arose. His friend who had good local knowledge, persuaded him to take up the job. Mark obliged and gave three months' notice to the Edinburgh firm to quit. Mark took up legal practice in Halifax in West Yorkshire and bought a house in the nearby Village of Sowerby Bridge.

3

The Wedding

The engagement was fixed in Colombo at St Mary's church. Pope Nicholas I defined espousal as 'pacts of promise of future marriage'. The betrothal is either a bilateral or unilateral contract since it is mutually agreed by both parties or made by one and accepted by the other party. St Thomas referred to the engagement as 'quasi-sacramental.'

Since the engagement was so closely allied with the Sacrament of Matrimony, it was most fitting that it took place in church, preferably at the communion railing. The Holy See did not permit the introduction of any new liturgical ceremonies on private authority.

The priest, vested in surplice and white stole, and with his assistants vested in surplice, awaited the couple at the communion table. As Jacob and Julie came forward with the two witnesses they had chosen, the antiphon and psalm were sung on the eighth psalm tone 'To the Lord I will tender my promise: in the presence of all His people.'

The priest then bid the couple to join their right hands, while they repeated after him the solemn declarations. Then the priest took the two ends of his stole and in the form of a cross placed them over the clasped hands of the couple. Holding the stole in place with his left hand, he said,

'I bear witness of your solemn proposal and I declare you betrothed. In the name of the Father, and of the Son, and of the

Holy Spirit. Amen.' As he was pronouncing the last words, he sprinkled them with holy water in the form of a cross. He blessed the engagement ring by sprinkling with holy water. Jacob took the ring and placed it first on the index finger of the left hand of Julie and said, 'In the name of the Father,' (then on the middle finger) 'and of the Son,' (finally placed and left it on the ring finger) 'and of the Holy Spirit.' The priest opened the missal at the beginning of the Canon and presented the page imprinted with the crucifixion to be kissed first by Jacob and then by Julie.

Following that, the engagement party was held at Pinto's house. He put up a marquee to accommodate 120 guests. Julie wore a light pink Ted Baker Celeyst v-neck georgette midi dress with matching pink Esperanza pump stilettoes. The dark toffee hair with pigeon wings at the temples formed luxurious foams of curls flowing over to her hips and loose ponytail at the base of the neck with a rose flower. The sapphire and diamond belle drop earrings in white gold were dazzling. Her perfume, La Vie Est Belle by Lancôme, taking its name from the phrase 'Life is beautiful,' was bursting with the invigorating scents of fresh flowers, fruity blackcurrant, pear, vanilla and praline.

Jacob was wearing a light grey slim fit blazer over a light blue striped shirt and burgundy silk tie and burgundy printed Oxfords patent leather fall comfort shoes. His hair cut was Elvis style, a traditional quaff which added volume to his hair. The sides were cut shorter while the hair on top was combed forward except the front part. The strands in the front were unevenly brushed up. With added hair wax, the hair glistened gloriously in the dazzling lights.

The party was held to celebrate the couple's engagement and to help future wedding guests get to know one another. As per tradition, the bride's parents hosted the engagement party. All had an amazing time at the party. Everybody socialized, danced and had a lot of fun throughout the evening. They were all elated with the celebrations and smiling faces all around.

Pinto and Lilly presented the couple with matching keyrings, which were perfectly sentimental gifts befitting the occasion. This was a small but lovely gift, as it meant they could add them to their car keys or house keys and they would be with them wherever they went, especially perfect if the happy couple are due to move into a new home together. Mark and Molly gave the couple a two-in-one ring box, a vow book and a jewellery box, a beautiful product designed to look like a classic romance novel. Inside the box there was space to store the vows and wedding rings both before and after the wedding day, a lovely thoughtful engagement gift idea. Pinto and Lilly followed the Catholic tradition *verbatim*.

Soon after, they made an appointment with the local parish priest to check he was willing to perform the ceremony, check the church was free on the date chosen, pay an initial deposit towards the church service being held, and the choir, and fill out a few forms giving the names and addresses for the legal publication of the wedding banns. This was to announce the intended marriage. The banns were published by being read aloud during the service on three successive Sundays preceding the ceremony. The congregation was invited to register any objections, if they had any.

Stage one was complete. So they progressed onto planning the wedding ceremony. The priest advised on all areas of the service and help with the choice of readings, psalms and hymns. The parish organist and choir were arranged. One of Jacob's friends, who was a guitarist, was chosen to play as well.

The wedding was at St Mary's Church, Colombo. The church was partly of gothic architecture with the top of the cross facing Jerusalem. The east end of the church was called the sanctuary and it contained the altar - a table where the bread and wine are blessed during the Eucharist, the lectern – a stand where the Bible was read from, the pulpit, where the priest delivered sermons, and a crucifix, a cross with Jesus on. There was a rail which acted to separate the sanctuary from the place where the congregations sat, known as the nave. In the nave there were many rows of pews where the congregation sat in rows on benches.

Across the church walls, there were 14 framed pictures, the Stations of the Cross, which showed the events of Jesus' crucifixion. There was a stoup, a small basin containing holy water which Catholics dip their hand in to make the sign of the cross to renew their baptism promises. There were statues of Christ, Mary, and various saints. The stained-glass windows depicted biblical stories and religious teachings. There were candles to be lit by the congregation when they were praying and an organ to be played during hymn singing.

The Catechism of the Catholic Church stated: 'The intimate community of life and love which constitutes the married state has been established by the Creator and endowed by him with its own proper laws. God himself is the author of marriage. The vocation to marriage is written in the very nature of man and woman as they came from the hand of the Creator. Marriage is not a purely human institution despite the many variations it may have undergone through the centuries in different cultures, social structures, and spiritual attitudes. These differences should not cause us to forget its common and permanent characteristics. Although the dignity of this institution is not transparent everywhere with the same clarity, some sense of the greatness of the matrimonial union exists in all cultures. The well-being of the individual person and of both human and

Christian society is tightly bound up with the healthy state of conjugal and family life.'

Julie was wearing an Alex Perry Maddison bridal gown. Crafted from white silk, the design had a fitted, triangle-cut bodice with delicate shoulder straps for a sweetly romantic look. Softly clinched at the waist, the graceful silhouette was finished with a full, floor-skimming pleated skirt with concealed side pockets. She was wearing Faith silver 'Del' block heel sandals. Her hair-do was a ballerina bun which sat higher up the head with a floral vine headband. Make-up was monochromatic nude hues blending with the hair colour to create a uniform appearance that showcased her stunning eyes. The glossy rose lipstick evoked a vintage vibe. She wore a silver pearl cubic zirconia drop pendant and earrings set. Like the traditional meaning of a white dress, pearls were meant to symbolize purity. People believed that wearing pearls on your wedding day would bring a happy marriage. Many brides do this hoping not to shed any tears in matrimony. Julie held a shower bouquet with multi-coloured roses and tulips, enhanced with trailing ivy and foliage, and looked the epitome of elegance and sophistication, designed to gracefully flow out of the bride's hands.

Jacob wore a royal blue Hawes & Curtis twill classic fit suit, matched with a red lapel flower. The white poplin slim fit tunic shirt and burgundy Salvatore Ferragamo anchor print silk tie stood out in sharp contrast. He had a Caesar Cut hairstyle, the top was about an inch longer than the rest of the hair. This style left a fringe on the forehead that was combed downward. The sides and back were not tapered. He wore black shoes which were Dr. Martens Adrian Tassel loafers.

Mark had specially hired a Rolls-Royce Phantom VIII for the wedding. It had a short front overhang and upright front end, a long bonnet and set-back passenger compartment as well as a long wheelbase and a flowing rear end. It also used rear-opening 'coach doors'. For the first time on a Phantom, Rolls-Royce's trademark 'Parthenon' radiator grille was integrated into the surrounding bodywork. He later told Pinto he was a lifelong Beatle fan and that John Lennon used a Romany gypsy wagon-style painted Rolls-Royce Phantom V.

The church was packed. The assembly stood. The entrance song was sung. The priest and servers' investments proper to the liturgy greeted the bridal party at the door of the church then all entered in procession as was customary for a Mass - the ministers first, followed by the priest, then the bride and bridegroom, proceeded by their parents and the two witnesses. The priest led the assembly in the sign of the cross after the entrance song was finished. The priest invited the couple to declare their consent to be married, which they did by stating their marriage vows. The priest blessed the wedding rings through prayer and the sprinkling of holy water. Jacob placed a white gold diamond Chanel set ring on Julie's finger, and Julie placed a white gold diamond two row band ring on Jacob's finger.

The wedding reception was held at Hotel Taj Intercontinental, a five-star venue. There were 120 guests. The menu was a five- course meal composed of (a) crisps with Fromager d'Affinois and Meyer Lemon ginger jelly (b) asparagus and 'drunken goats' cheese soup (c) chicken thighs over mashed potatoes and cauliflower with Tarragon Quadrello di Bufala cream sauce and steamed carrots (d) semi-sweet chocolate stilton mousse with freshly whipped cream and pomegranate (e) tea and coffee with biscuits.

The Master of Ceremony announced, 'Ladies and gentlemen, the speeches and toasts will begin in five minutes, so if there is something that you have to attend to or if you need to powder your face, please do it soon.'

'The first toast tonight, and what may be considered the most important, is the toast to the bride and groom and this honour and responsibility falls well on the shoulders of the father of the bride, Mark.

Mark introduced himself and started clearing his throat with a joke. 'I am only allowed five minutes because of my throat. If I go on too long my wife has threatened to get at my throat.' The ripple of laughter from the crowd brightened the mood. In a sombre mood he said, 'Ladies and gentlemen, may I ask all of you to stand up and let us observe a few moments silence in memory of the people we lost in the Tsunami?' Then with a sarcastic smile, he remarked, 'Don't forget the countless carnations, lilies and roses who selflessly gave their lives to make this wedding celebration possible.'

He welcomed the guests and thanked the bridesmaids and wedding party. He expressed special gratitude to Molly, Pinto and Lilly. Mark got emotional when he narrated that he cried when Julie went backpacking to Venezuela for a month during her holiday after finishing her university examinations.

He welcomed Jacob officially as the son-in-law and said he was looking forward to working with him as a new family member. Then, he turned towards Jacob and quipped, 'Will I continue to have to mow the lawn myself every weekend?' He went on pass some words of wisdom to the couple. 'Whenever you're wrong, admit it. Whenever you are right, keep quiet.' He ended with the Biblical quote, **'**Be kind and compassionate to one another, forgiving each other, just as God forgave you. Ephesians 4:32.'

Finally, for toasting the couple, he asked all to stand up and raise their glasses. After Mark's speech, a series of speeches followed.

The MC announced, 'And now comes the cutting of that beautiful cake. So, I would like Julie and Jacob to walk around to the front of the bridal table to perform their first duty as husband and wife.'

As they approached the cake, the MC commented, 'It is a shame that we actually have to destroy this beautiful piece of art by cutting it but it would be a greater shame if we left it uneaten.'

The wedding cake was three-layered with pillar supports. It was a masterpiece of culinary science in its own right - exuberant, elegant and theatrical. The bottom tier was filled with chocolate custard. The middle tier was intricately crafted profiteroles, each thinly encrusted with hard-crack sugar, filled with pastry cream, with glistening strands of caramel and chocolate. The top tier was chocolate cake covered with lustrous white chocolate marzipan roses and dusted over lightly with golden powder. The smiling couple was the 'topper' figure.

With the bride closest to the cake and the groom behind her, he placed both hands onto the knife, cut an inch into the cake and sliced down cleanly. Then he made a connecting cut for a wedge, using the cake knife to lift the wedge out and onto the plate. Cake cutting is the last 'official' event of the evening. It is a signal for those who are not awfully close to show that they can leave. A few guests started leaving.

Due to his in-depth knowledge of music, Mark had already selected the songs for wedding dance. They were 'You are the Best Thing' by Ray Lamontagne, 'Make you feel My Love' by Adele, 'Better Together' by Jack Johnson, 'Can't Help Falling in Love' by Elvis Presley and 'Thinking Out Loud' by Ed Sheeran.

The party carried on. The younger generation took over. The parents – all the four withdrew from the chaos by about 8.30 at night. Lilly and Molly went together to talk about forward planning of things.

Mark told Pinto, 'I have a plan. Let us take a private room now. Shall I tell Molly and Lilly that we have some things to discuss regarding Jacob's visa, job and other matters and not to disturb us?'

So they went upstairs. Mark opened up, 'I have been waiting all my life for this day. I am sure you too feel the same. Let us get drunk.' Both stood up, did a high-five, took their ties off and loosened up. They buzzed for the waiter who arrived promptly. Pinto ordered whisky glasses, liquor sprout, ice, soda, ginger ale and titbits and pickles.

Mark had brought Glenturret from England precisely marked for this occasion - 'The secret summit of the dads of newlyweds.' He handed over the bottle to Pinto to open it and started giving a vivid description of its origin. 'Glenturret is a town lying east of Trossachs in Scotland, a gentle landscape of wooded hills and peaceful lochs. It came from Scotland's oldest distillery, founded in 1775.'

Pinto was about to pour the whisky in the glasses. Mark asked him to put the sprout on to avoid any spills. He quipped, 'We don't want to spill any drops as tax to the angel or devil.' They stood up, raised and clinked glasses and said, 'Cheers for the newlyweds, mums and dads and to all.'

Mark joked, 'At the railway crossing it says "Listen, Look and Cross with care". Here I say "Smell, Look and Drink with enjoyment".' Mark continued expressing his expert knowledge in whisky terms. 'This is 29 years old, single malt, 55.6% ABV, single cask, delicate nose, fragrant, with lemonade and vanilla, floral on palate, with hay, honey and spicy oak, and wood tannins. The finish is medium in length with toffee and developing oak.'

'Let us get drunk and tell each other everything we are too afraid to say when sober.' Mark broadcast the mission statement.

Pinto nodded twice in full approval.

Pinto quipped, 'You don't really know someone until you get ridiculously drunk with them.'

'Drink alcohol because no good story ever started with someone eating salad.' Mark responded in style.

Pinto made a philosophical point. 'The drunk mind speaks the sober heart.'

Both laughed; they were already getting tipsy.

Mark, while refilling the glasses, cracked a joke. 'In my younger days, I used to think that drinking was bad; so I totally gave up thinking.'

Pinto paused for a couple of seconds and retorted in style, 'Everyone needs to believe in something; I believe we should have another drink soon.'

Pinto walked up to the window and drew the curtains. There was still some natural light. The sun was about to set. He called Mark towards the window to enjoy the sunset. There was a silky, smooth collusion of sky burst reds and yellows into the calm of night. It was a symphony of colours as it sent all to serene sleep, a great delight stirring the souls.

They went to the nearby beach for a walk to take a mini-break and get some fresh air. As they strolled, the unruly waves crashed across the jagged landscape stroking and caressing their bare feet. When the waves receded, the crabs and turtles were visible actively seeking shelters. The lapping waves led to encroaching tides. They stood still, observing the ebbs and flows. The flock of birds were conducting choreographed dance, singing swan songs for the day in harmony with the surges and recedes.

In the far corner, the serial silhouette shadows of the distant dark-blue mountains against the backdrop of the crimson-red sky, gave a glorified image of a stepladder to the other mysterious world beyond. The giant crispy circle of sun hesitantly dipped into the ocean smiling and waving at the waves a wavering goodbye. The dipping sun spat at the day spilling symphonically a cocktail of colours - orange, grey, blue and black. The ocean swallowed the mighty sun with a greedy gulp. While walking, Pinto noted a dead seabird, which was a bad omen since flight gave the birds youth, wisdom, and divinity. Distracting Mark's attention, Pinto suggested they return to the hotel.

They went back to the hotel room. Pinto poured another round of drinks. He put his left elbow on the windowsill, rested his head on his head and pointed to the south-east and sighed in reminiscence 'You can see a tiny bit of that white building; that was my garment factory. I used to produce garments and hand-painted fabrics. There was a lot of demand from Iran, Dubai and China.'

Mark took another sip and veered in that direction inquisitively. He felt his head was buzzing. Pinto continued.

'When I started thirty years back, I had only five women workers - two needlewomen, a cutter, seamstress and a designer. I took a bank loan to start the business. Slowly the market picked up.'

Mark loosened his shirt buttons and eagerly listened, trying to resist the attempts of his eyelids to shut down the eyes. He looked hammered.

'Within five years I made a lot of money. The export was great. When I sold the factory after 25 years, there were 40 employees. I made a good fortune.' He narrated his success story with immense pride and joy.

Both sat down on the settee.

Mark started in a sombre mood, 'When I came to England thirty years back, though I had a law degree, I had to get another qualification to practice. Fortunately, I got into a big firm as a trainee. The senior partner was a kind and benevolent man. He helped me a lot to go up in my career.'

Pinto interjected inquisitively. 'What about Jacob's job prospects?'

'He will need to do a qualifying examination. But I have got all the backup, no worries.' Mark's speech started slurring.

Pinto was plastered, unsteady and asked Mark to give him a hand to get to the toilet.

They both were sloshed and decided to call it a day.

4

Passage to England

As soon as Mark got back to England, he prepared the relevant documents and sent them across to Pinto in Sri Lanka. He and Jacob went to the British High Commission in Colombo to get the entry visa to the UK.

Hasty preparations for the trip got underway. Pinto started talking to him in 'father to son' mode regarding dealing with his newlywed wife and the in-laws. Since Pinto had travelled abroad many times, he gave an overview of international travel, foreign customs, and manners. Lilly got busy making lime pickles and sweets. She did them with utmost care and delicacy so that her signature was stamped on the preparations as a living testament to her culinary skills. Jacob started saying farewell to his friends.

Being the first flight, Pinto had gone through all the procedures with Jacob and he prepared a check list in his pocket. After getting ready at home, they said a common prayer especially to Saint Christopher, the Patron Saint of Travellers. Pinto went through the list - baggage, passport, flight ticket, other documents, credit cards etc. All were in order. He ensured that the belly luggage was locked and secured in the case, to avoid being tampered on the way.

Flying for the first time, especially an international flight, Jacob was filled with sheer joy and excitement. He brushed up his knowledge about flying. In 1903, Americans Orville and Wilbur Wright completed the world's first successful controlled powered flight at Kill Devil Hills near Kitty Hawk, North Carolina. Pinto and Lilly set off to see Jacob off. When the car got out of the gate, Jacob turned his head back towards the house and kept staring till it disappeared from his eyeline. He felt a profound sense of loss leaving his home and parents who were the rocks supporting every movement of his life.

His mind travelled fast, figuring out the challenging transitions of a new woman, the wife taking care of him and his household. A residual uneasy silence lingered in the car. To dispel the awkwardness, Lilly quipped,

'Emirates is probably the best airline in the world, fantastic service, excellent food and plenty of music channels.' That flattery put a broad smile on Jacob's face.

He exclaimed, 'Are all the food and drinks free?'

Pinto intercepted jovially, 'Everything is free; make the most of it.'

They parked the car, got a baggage trolley and accompanied him to the departure lounge. Jacob joined the check-in queue for the Emirates Flight to Dubai. He checked in the baggage and got the tag for hand luggage and the boarding pass. When he got his first ever boarding pass in his hand, he smiled, kissed it and put it in his pocket. Pinto and Molly gave him embraces and kisses and said goodbye. Jacob started his solitary solemn sojourn. He took his first steps towards his 8681 Km travel to Manchester. His heart was beating faster, he felt dizzy, and the spittle become congealed. He went through the immigration and security checks and reached the duty-free stores. He clarified that it meant the items were free of local or national taxes. He browsed around the glittering row of shops with smiling beautiful girls trying to earn their commission by canvassing the products to buy. Pinto had already told him that there would be four hours gap in Dubai and that the shops there are much bigger and world-famous. So, Jacob strolled through into the waiting lounge at a leisurely pace as an onlooker.

He went to the bar and got a Seventh Heaven Cocktail as an icebreaker for his epic journey ahead. That composed of Angostura bitters, maraschino, caper tiff and dry gin. He found a scenic vantage point and sat down to enjoy his drink and take photos of the hectic schedules of a multitude of people of all nationalities passing by him.

He saw the Emirates Boeing 777 destined to take him from the waiting lounge. A sudden influx of goose pimples circulated through him. He checked Google to find out more about the plane. 'The Boeing 777-300 is a long range, twin aisle, twin-engine jet manufactured by Boeing, the American aerospace company, often referred to as the 'Triple Seven'. It was the world's first commercial aircraft entirely designed solely by computer. The capacity is 550.'

He started clicking selfies at the airport, took pictures of the boarding pass and sent it to Molly and Julie and a few of his close friends. He wanted to show the world a definitive proof of his sojourn. He did a happy dance as soon as the flight status confirmation was displayed, triggering an exhilarating level of excitement.

Then he was stung with fear like a flea bite. 'What if there is something wrong with my documents? Molly had kept some home-made lime pickle in the case; what if they find that in my luggage? Oh my god! If somebody hijacks the plane… I can't think…' Jacob started sweating.

Suddenly, a team of teenage girls in sports uniform was rushing past him giggling which caught his attention. They were going to New Delhi to take part in a hockey tournament. The periodic airport announcements interrupting the light background music, the hustle-bustle and screaming children, all gave an aura of a new world of fun and fervour.

The period between check-in and waiting to board the flight was although bit dragging but it was more intriguing and inquisitive. For Jacob who was flying for the first time, it was testing his patience to wait for those minutes to pass. He kept watching the display of boarding and departures on the screen like a hawk. He went to the cloakroom, relieved himself. He freshened himself up, brushed his teeth, put on face powder, combed his hair and caressed his pencil shaped moustache. He rehearsed the smile twice. 'Ah, I look handsome.' He took a refreshing sigh and walked back to the waiting lounge.

Then came the announcement he had been waiting for 'Passengers for Emirates Flight EK 361 to Dubai, kindly proceed to Gate 18.' Like a whining schoolboy carrying his schoolbag, he picked up his brief case and walked majestically with an upright back, stiff neck and tilted head. On getting into the aircraft, two smiling, beautiful air hostesses welcomed him, standing on either side of the entry. He could not fathom out who was more beautiful, although he scanned his eyes both ways twice in succession. He made the verdict in ten seconds, the lady on the right was bit more beautiful, but it was only 51 to 49 percent – a very narrow margin. He reached his seat, which was towards the rear of the aircraft.

The lulling melody of Mozart's 'Four Seasons' was soothing. The sight of hundreds of passengers joining him made him feel a bit easier. After a brief moment of happiness, flashing thoughts of crashes and hijacks crossed his mind. The crew completed all pre-flight checks. The cabin doors were closed. The First Officer announced that the flight would be departing soon.

The plane's engines were designed to move it forward at high speed. They made air flow rapidly over the wings, which threw the air down toward the ground, generating an upward force called lift that overcame the plane's weight. The wings forced the air downward and that pushed the plane upward into the air and the plane took off smoothly. The pilot announced everything was okay, the flight time to Dubai was 3 hours and 50 minutes and the weather condition was sunny. Jacob took a deep sigh of relief, unbuckled his seat belt and thanked God. He looked outside through the window. He was in the sky, unharmed and with an exceptional view of the clouds and blue sky. It felt surreal, beautiful, and refreshing. After about 15 minutes, when he looked out, he saw the emerald Arabian Sea in which stood isolated groups of islands with pristine white sandy beaches, incredible coral reefs and clusters of palm trees.

Dried fruits and nuts were served. When there was a bit of turbulence, Jacob felt uncomfortable and scared. The lady sat next to him sensed it. She just smiled and enquired,

'Are you ok?'

Jacob admitted he was a novice to flying. Soon she started chatting. She was Olivia, a 25-year-old American, a United Nations officer returning from a project visit to Sri Lanka after a week. Jacob saw her slowly peering through the seat numbers and when she sat next to him, he was gobsmacked by her beauty. His first impression was that she had a blessed body with curious curves, heavenly hips, and thunderous thighs.

She looked like a goddess of the sun. Her golden hair draped down softly curling along the ends. Every time she talked, her smile never faded, and Jacob felt that time never ended. She was a siren of sudden happiness. The beauty in her blue eyes was deep like the ocean. She did scent-marking like a lioness with a delicate, piquant, evocative fragrance emanating from her and lingering on as detached clouds in their eclipse of their seats.

She was wearing a black square neck ruched mesh bodycam

dress which broadcast her astounding body curves. Jacob felt he was sitting next to a stunning beauty. Although he had planned to listen to music during the journey, he could not take his eyes off her. She was explaining that her job involved frequent transatlantic air travel to various continents. She had already travelled to Asia, Africa, and South America many times. Jacob thought, 'My goodness, she has been around the world many times. This is my very first flight.' In a few minutes the plane got into an air pocket causing bit of turbulence. Suddenly, due to fear, a feverish tremor shook Jacob's frame. Olivia sensed the sentiments which actuated him and tried to reassure him.

Since she was very much touched by the poverty and suffering of the people in Sri Lanka, her plan was to make some pragmatic recommendations to provide basic sanitation, water supply and financial incentives for poor social class and small businesses. Being intrigued by her zest and concern for the poor, Jacob gave her a long and questioning look. They chatted energetically.

The air hostess came around serving drinks. Jacob had a double Glenmorangie scotch whisky while Olivia picked a red wine from a selection of three. He noted the label 'Cabernet Shiraz Passion Has Red Lips.' Jacob enquired why she chose that wine. She gave an instant description 'It is full-bodied Australian blend. Also, it is vegan, tasty and sustainable.' Taking his eyes off her, he took a long swallow of his whisky, and with an admiring smile switched his eyes back to her. Her untarnished glistening white teeth sparkled like pearls while she chatted.

Out of ignorance and anticipatory anxiety, Jacob enquired about how to find a connecting flight in Dubai. She gave a vivid description of the procedures on landing since she had been to Dubai many times. She reiterated that the connecting flight would not leave without him since his baggage had already been checked in direct to Manchester. He felt reassured.

Shortly afterwards, the delicious food arrived. It was Teriyaki salmon with sesame pak choi, baked new potatoes with rosemary and sea salt, a bread roll with butter, a salad tray with sliced tomatoes, cucumber and lettuce, Cheese slices with olives, and bread and butter pudding. The colourful display of the food intrigued Jacob. He took a few pictures of the food tray on his mobile as a memoir of his first ever plane food. It was followed by tea and coffee.

A few minutes later, the air hostess came with the duty free trolley. Jacob was told by Pinto to do his shopping at Dubai airport. Olivia scanned through the perfumes and picked a perfume called 'La Prairie Silver Rain'. She paid by credit card, left the bottle on the seat, and soon rushed to the toilet in haste. Jacob noticed a card on the floor. It was her UN identity card with her photo and date of birth. He noted her date of birth, 11 November. He took it and returned it to her when she came back. She thanked him and said that it might have slipped from her bag while paying the air hostess. She went on, 'This perfume is for my mum. She always prefers things bought on the plane. This is a Swiss perfume developed after being inspired by Alps Mountains, where rain transforms into attractive icy crystals and fall from 1,000 feet, very spectacular sight. That is why it is called Silver Rain.'

Shortly afterwards, the announcement came that the flight would be landing in 15 minutes. Olivia gave her business card to Jacob. Since he did not have one, he wrote down his details for her. The flight landed in Dubai and they bid farewell.

There was a 4 hour and 10 minute gap for the connecting flight to Manchester. Jacob proceeded to the transit lounge. He felt he was in a dazzling magical world, seeing the enormity of the airport. He sat down and googled Dubai airport.

Dubai International Airport is a major aviation hub not only in the UAE but also in the whole world. The city of Dubai is obsessed with luxe and wealth. It is the fastest-growing aviation hub in the world, allowing 87 million passengers through it. The airport provides modern infrastructure and services and manages connections between 260 destinations worldwide. It is a transit zone for more than 100 airlines with terminals equipped with modern facilities and the best lounges.

Emirates is considered as one of the best airlines in the world. This is why its main hub has the same level of service and facilities. Terminal 3 is entirely dedicated to these airlines for more comfort of their prestigious passengers. The Emirates business class lounge is an entire world of entertainment. Besides countless information desks, there are staff members with 'May I help you' T-shirts. The airport has its own five-star hotel inside its building. If anybody is exhausted from a long flight, he can get some rest in the Dubai International hotel situated in Terminal 1 which offers swimming pool, restaurants, and a conference hall. The structure also provides tiny rooms in its Snooze Cube hotel to take a few hours of sleep. There is no need to worry about missing the connecting flight since the staff will give a call if needed. The airport has its own Zen Gardens located in Terminal 3 and it is heaven to escape from the heavy noise of this busy airport, to get some rest and just relax in a natural environment before the connecting flight.

The Dubai Airport is quite big to welcome the A380 aircrafts. The Concourse A of Terminal 3 is dedicated to the giant Airbus A380 aircraft. It was opened in 2013 for this purpose to ensure the simultaneous boarding of more than 800 passengers at a time. The airport uses underground trains and tunnels to connect the Concourse A to the other parts of the building.

The airport employs more than 90,000 people. Currently, the city ensures its development by tourism revenues. There are smart gates. The residents of the United Arab Emirates can pass through smart gates with their Emirates ID. In this way, they will skip queues without sacrificing valuable time.

For shopping, Pinto had given his son plenty of money to spare to impress his bride and family. The duty-free store was the biggest; the shopping capital of the world. Jacob bought a strawberry red vintage Emmons three-heart necklace for Julie, a bottle of Tobermory 32-year-old single malt whisky for Mark and perfume for Molly - L'interdit Givenchy, the modern version of the iconic L'interdit, one of the best creations of Givenchy and a tribute to freedom and 'bold femininity'.

Jacob had a 'Kicker' cocktail composed of vermouth, calvados and Bacardi rum. Sipping the drink, and leaning on the settee, he put his hand baggage and the bag of gifts close to him and gazed at all the hustle and bustle around him. The airport terminal was a remarkably busy place of hectic happenings. With many passengers coming in and many others leaving, there was a constant movement of both people and planes. From the waiting area, there was a clear glimpse of the runway. Many people enjoyed looking through the glass, watching the planes land and take-off. It was almost a magical experience especially for children.

An Emirates Airlines flight was just landing. Though it was quite fast, and the sun was setting, the company insignia was clearly visible. Then parts of its wings were raised to slow it down. As the plane slowed down considerably, it glided from one end of the runway to the far corner.

With so many planes landing, it was difficult to keep track of that one plane continuously. When announcements were made, many who were asleep were woken up by their family members.

Those who were reading, quickly put their reading material in the baggage. People had formed long queues near the designated boarding gates. Everyone had their hand baggage with them and their boarding passes in their hand, ready for inspection by officials. An announcement was made to allow senior citizens, expecting mothers and ladies with children, to board the plane. Everyone made way for them. An elderly lady was being pushed by her son at speed since he had been in toilet when the announcement came.

As the staff at the counter checked the boarding passes, mobile staircases were attached to the front and the rear doors of the plane. A fleet of buses rolled in. People got into the buses. Some sat, while others stood, holding on the handles and bars for support, with most peering eagerly through the gaps gazing at the herd of aircrafts lying still and patiently. The buses drove right up to the airplane. The passengers disembarked from the buses and boarded the flight. In the distance, many more flights were seen landing.

Jacob felt like it was a trip to the moon. Once he got in, he studied this manmade marvel by checking Google. The two-storey A380 has a maximum take-off weight of 575 tonnes – that is about five blue whales. It is the largest passenger airliner in the world and when launched, airports had to upgrade their facilities to accommodate the giant. It has 40% more usable space than the second largest plane – the Boeing 747 A380 can provide seating for up to 853 passengers. It has a total flying range of 15,200 km which means that it's used to service two of the longest non-stop flights in the world, Auckland to Dubai and Dallas/Fort Worth to Sydney. Emirates Airlines has the most A380s in their fleet – 94 plus 12 on order. With infrastructure struggling to keep up with demand for landing slots and airport gates, the superjumbo allows the airline to increase passenger volume with fewer aircraft and fewer flights. Emirates sends nine A380 flights from Dubai to London every day. The first ever airline to have an A380 in their fleet was Singapore Airlines who started flying it in 2007. At the airport, other airplanes have to wait up to three minutes before they can start their take-off after an A380 due to the wake turbulence from its four engines and wingtips. The price of one Airbus A380 is a whopping 445 million US dollars. It takes 34 people working fulltime for 15 days to repaint one A380. It is a pan-European product; the engines and wings are produced in England, parts of the fuselage and the tail in Germany and Spain. Airbus test engineer, Fernando Alonso, described the airplane as 'a symbol of Europe.' When complete, these airplane sections are shipped by land, air, and sea for final assembly in France.

The Airbus A380's wings are the biggest ever created, wingspan 79.75 meters, 2,775 square feet in size and 54 percent larger than the wings of a Boeing 747. What a progression – the Wright Brothers' first flight was shorter than the A380's wingspan. The A380 is 24.1 meters high, 72.7 meters long, equivalent to the length of two blue whales. The plane is propelled by four Rolls-Royce Trent 900 engines.

After reading about all the intricate details of this sky giant, Jacob felt overwhelmed and shed a few tears. He had a detailed read of the in-flight menu and took it as a souvenir.

Beverages
Cold drinks A selection of juices and soft drinks
Hot drinks Coffee and tea
From the bar A range of red and white wine, beer, spirits and liqueurs
Or treat yourself to a little extra:
Moët & Chandon Brut 200ml for USD 20

All our meals are halal.
We're sorry if occasionally your meal choice isn't available.

Light bites
Snacks Emirates pizza
Vegetarian pizza topped with tomatoes, melted cheese and oregano
Fruit and snack bars
Available between meal services

Dinner
Appetiser sweet potato and bean salad
Main course grilled chicken
With sundried tomato pesto, mashed potatoes and seasonal vegetables
Paneer makhani
Served with cumin rice with raisins and cashew nuts

Dessert
Strawberry yoghurt mousse
Topped with strawberry compote

Breakfast
Appetiser fresh seasonal fruit
Main course classic omelette
Served with spiced potato wedges,
sautéed mushrooms and spinach
Aloo methi
Sautéed potatoes with fenugreek leaves,
served with vegetable cutlets and cumin paratha
Bread croissant
Served with butter and preserve

Jacob chatted with various air hostesses – Lebanese, Indian, Chinese, and English. He made sure to take selfies and sign autographs with every hostess he could liaise with, to add to his memorabilia of his maiden long-haul flight. He slept for about a couple of hours.

The plane landed in Manchester at seven in the morning. Mark was waiting; he picked him up at the airport. It was November time. While walking towards the car, Jacob could feel the chill as the lungs filled with sharp frosty air each time he breathed in. He had the first glimpse of an English autumn.

While crossing the Pennines, he was curious to see the snow covering the top of the mountains, looking like nature's winter hat covering the green canopy. The darkish grey clouds were loitering lazily, producing a rainbow while the sun was attempting to break through the gaps. Approaching the house, the feast of fallen leaves littered the roads, left alone to decay, and die like unwanted progenies after shading and illuminating the trees for almost half the year. Jacob thought, when the dry leaves fall, the green leaves laugh.

While Mark parked the car in the driveway, Jacob was struck with stunning silence looking at the porch which was covered by the pendulous racemes hanging down forming a colourful curtain of scented lilac-blue flowers, the elegant dense foliage of bright green pinnate leaves, the jaw-dropping drooping seed pods and the girly gnarled trunks with twisted branches of the mysterious wisteria. The scattered petals on the ground appeared like snowflakes or cornflakes spilt by a naughty toddler on the kitchen floor. The pair of hanging baskets were heavily pregnant with Surfinia white petunia, pelargonium and trailing ivy sticking out against the backdrop of the brick wall, on either side of the door.

Julie was waiting in the lounge, pacing back and forth

impatiently. On seeing Jacob, she pulled her hands out of the pocket of her jeans and tossed up her mane of thick black hair, her soft eyes lit up like flash bulbs and she thrust herself with a thud onto him giving him an almighty embrace. Looking at the fire burning in the hearth like bonfire, Jacob exclaimed,

'My goodness, I felt freezing when I landed. The temperature in Sri Lanka when I left was 34 degrees.'

The house had been hastily refurbished after the wedding with sheer speed and ruthless efficiency. That was the wedding gift from Mark and Molly. The lounge appeared more spacious and elegant. Julie was in sole charge of the makeover of her bedroom. The bedroom had a high ceiling and a wide, curved bay window which overlooked the back garden. Julie changed the maroon wallpaper to a mural roll romantic purple tree Wall background. Jacob had a quick shower and breakfast. Due to jet lag, Julie took him straight upstairs. On walking into the bedroom, Jacob's eyes lit up, he took a deep sigh and stood astounded, amazed and astonished in the salacious transformation and presentation of the room compared to what he envisaged in the photographs he had seen prior to the wedding. The fragrance, Light Blue by Dolce and Gabbana, was infused into the scented candles, which gave a mesmerizing ambience.

The kingsize bed was dressed in a pink rose print Camas Shabby Chic bedspread, personalized pillows with 'Jacob' and 'Julie' stitched on them and an Afghan red and white polka dot throw to set the most romantic, relaxing, and rejuvenating tone. The two Chinese lamps at each bedside set up the mood lighting. Wedding photographs - in five different poses hung on the wall smiling at them. There was a vase with a bunch of red roses.

Julie looked into his eyes and murmured, 'My waiting felt like eternity.' He enveloped her in his arms and caressed her gently.

The sudden rush of love surged through her like a storm changing her into a volcano of exploding passion. He lifted her onto the bed and started kissing her fervently and passionately, intermittently gasping to take fresh bouts of breath. She returned slow, deep, and passionate kisses on his lips, while her hands caressed the tendrils of his black hair. His heart was pounding, tears of joy trickled down Jacob's cheeks spilling onto Julie's cheeks like little rivulets, smudging her makeup. The sudden rush of blood led to instant arousal and loss of control of all inhibitions, and they sank onto the bed for the sojourn. Jacob slept through till ten at night.

The next day, Julie took Jacob for a drive out into the Pennine Hills, the range of hills and mountains separating northwest England from Yorkshire and northeast England. This was often described as the 'backbone of England', placed at 2800 feet above mean sea level. They went for a walk in the country park.

Jacob sighed, 'Back in Colombo, the street was so humid, dusty and noisy. It is nice to breathe the clean air and enjoy the loveliness of the countryside.'

The gentle breeze triggered an avalanche of golden yellow and dry brown leaves, leaving calling cards on Jacob and Julie as if they were being welcomed with a shower of flower petals. The pathways were gravelled and lined with deciduous trees. The sky was blue with thin pale clouds drifting aimlessly. The beams of sunlight were shining on them intermittently as they walked through the park. They noticed a loving pair of cardinal birds on a fig tree polishing their beaks tenderly. The wind got noisy, and the tree branches waved fiercely wanting to caress each other. Jacob felt quite chilly. So Julie decided to drive back.

The next week, Julie took him to Manchester. Located at the core of a vibrant city centre, The Arndale Centre, has been an icon of northwest shopping for three decades capturing 40 million visitors annually. Already a successful and much-loved shopping centre with heaps on offer, it was made better by creating a brand new food quarter giving people another reason to stay even longer. The new modern casual dining destination, Halle Place, has ten restaurants and cafés with stylish seating in a striking atrium. The enhanced dining scene fully complemented the centre's outstanding retail mix, giving customers an all-round, compelling experience. But this iconic centre also bears the sorrowful scars of past atrocity. In 1996, the Provisional Irish Republican Army detonated a 1,500 kilogram lorry bomb on Corporation Street near the centre.

After dinner they went to the Odeon Cinema. They saw the movie *Titanic*. The centrepiece of the film was the supreme and passionate love between Jack and Rose, who were from deeply contrasting social classes. Seventeen-year-old Rose hailed from an aristocratic family and was set to be married. On the ship, she met Jack Dawson, an artist, and fell in love with him. *RMS Titanic* was the most luxurious passenger ship which left Southampton in 1912 with a full set of passengers aboard. It was hailed as 'The unsinkable.'

Almost nearing the final leg of an epic journey, near Newfoundland coast, the ship struck a monster of an iceberg about 400 feet long and 100 feet above waterline, weighing millions of tons at a speed of 20.5 knots. It scraped the starboard on the right side of the hull producing a big gash which opened six watertight doors and water started filling in breaching the integrity. After fighting to survive for almost three hours, 'the unsinkable' iconic giant sank. Jack, who was in love with Rose, saved her life heroically. Their romance during the voyage became a classic romance all over the world. He died after professing his eternal love for Rose.

The Cunard Liner *RMS Carpathia* arrived at the scene two hours later and saved a few survivors floating in lifeboats. Thousands of scattered ice floes poignantly and painfully pointed to the 1,517 people who perished in the disaster. After seeing the movie which touched their hearts, they ended up embracing and kissing each other with tears of sorrow, love and joy.

The next day they went to Chester Zoo. Walking around, they saw a family of elephants congregating. Since in Sri Lanka, Jacob grew up with elephants, he knew a lot more about them. He narrated,

'Joy is an emotion that elephants love to show others. They express their happiness and display joy when they are playing and greeting friends or family members. During the birth of the new baby, the excitement of several of the females of family cannot be contained as they keep bellowing and blaring. Maybe they are making wide announcements to the outside world of the new arrival.' The calf was so small that it walked under its mother, who did not step on it or trip over it. Mother and child remained in constant touch. The mother often touched her child with her trunk and legs, helping it to its feet with one foot and her trunk. She pushed it under her to protect it. In a few minutes, she bathed it. With her trunk she collected water from the waterhole and sprayed over it and then scrubbed it gently. The mother steered her calf by grasping its tail with her trunk, and the calf followed holding its mother's tail.

Jacob went on. 'An elephant reunion is a highly emotional occasion. This joyful meeting between related, but separated, elephants is one of exuberance and drama. The greeting ceremony marks the incredible welcoming of a formerly absent family member. During the extraordinary event, the elephants about to be united begin calling each other. As they get closer, their pace quickens. Their excitement visibly flows as fluid from their temporal glands streams down the sides of their faces. Eventually, the elephants make a run towards each other, screaming and trumpeting the whole time. When they finally make contact, they form a loud, rumbling mass of flapping ears, clicked tusks and entwined trunks. The two lean on each other, rub each other, spin around and even defecate and urinate (what elephants do when they are experiencing sheer delight). With heads held high, the reunited pair fill the air with a symphony of trumpets, rumbles, screams, and roars.'

5

Honeymoon

The honeymoon for ten days across Europe was planned with meticulous precision by Mark. It was kept as a surprise to the newlyweds. Mark's idea was they should travel by all the three modes - land, air, and sea.

To start the trip, Mark drove them to Hull port. They boarded the P&O Ferry to Amsterdam to experience crossing the North Sea with an unrivalled level of service and entertainment.

The onboard services were excellent with a wide range of activities. For a classy dining experience, they went to The Brasserie, an exclusive à la carte restaurant which offered an unbeatable selection of food and soft and alcoholic drinks. There was a choice of five onboard bars offering a wide variety of different experiences. They went to the Sunset Show Bar and danced to live music for a couple of hours. After feeling tired, they proceeded to the Irish Bar to chill out with a bottle of champagne and catch up with the latest sports fixture on TV. By the time they got back to their en-suite cabin, it was 2.30 in the morning. They soon slipped into a deep sleep.

They reached Amsterdam by seven in the morning. Amsterdam is one of the most energetic, eclectic and exciting cities in Western Europe. They took a guided tour of the Heineken Museum, sampled the beer, and then visited the van Gogh Museum. Vincent Willem van Gogh was a Dutch post-impressionist painter who was among the most famous and influential figures in the history of western art. In just over a decade, he created about 2,100 artworks. The Anne Frank House was a writer's house and biographical museum dedicated to Jewish wartime diarist Anne Frank. The building was located on a canal called the Prinsengracht in central Amsterdam.

On day three, they took a train to Cologne in Germany. They went around the important tourist attractions. Cologne, a 2,000-year-old city spanning the Rhine River is the region's cultural hub. It is a landmark of high gothic architecture set amid a reconstructed old town. The magnificent Cologne Cathedral can be seen from nearly every point in the city centre and from many places elsewhere. It hovers above the roofs and chimneys of the city. It is not only used as a point of orientation but is the pride of the people in Cologne. The panorama of the city has been dominated by the cathedral's gigantic pair of towers. Museum Ludwig houses a collection of modern art. It includes works from Pop Art, Abstract and Surrealism, and has one of the largest Picasso collections in Europe. It holds many works by Andy Warhol and Roy Lichtenstein.

On day four, they went on a Rhine tour. Encompassing three of Europe's most famous waterways - the Danube, Main and Rhine - the leisurely cruise presented picturesque riverscapes at every bend. They enjoyed a sumptuous breakfast on deck. Sailing the most famous stretch, the beautiful Lorelei Passage was a poignant romantic journey. In between sails, they wandered wide-eyed through world-famous cities - Budapest, Amsterdam and Vienna - and strolled through the winding village streets in Miltenberg, Wertheim and Rüdesheim.

Winding through the heart of Eastern Europe, the magnificent Danube starts in Germany and makes its way into the Black Sea flowing through a staggering ten countries including Vienna, Romania and Hungary – the depth and diversity of each destination was awe-inspiring. The cruise offered a relaxed and informal way of experiencing the continually changing scenery from pretty medieval towns dotted along the riverbank to spectacular gorges fringed by mountain ranges.

They saw albatrosses - the large seabirds found in the Southern Ocean and the North Pacific regions. They are the largest flying birds with the longest wingspans of around 12 feet. They take almost ten years to mature and to start a relationship. The selection of partners among this species is an interesting process. They will not rush into any relationships; rather they learn the procedures that elders follow. They will learn dancing, staring, preening and vocalizations from them. After they will start dancing with many partners until they choose a special one for their entire life.

The pair then creates their own unique language and loving rituals. The couples will make themselves apt for the enormous process of egg-laying and chick-rearing. They usually build the nest in a near place of their native. Albatross lay one egg at a time and once the feathers grow for the chick, parents will fly off. After the search for food, they will come back occasionally.

The specialty of these unique birds is their love for their partners. They choose the partner and mate for entire life. Yes, they believe in their pair bond and show what real devoted love should be. Their entire life, endurance, and wisdom are fairly good enough; it is the real, so-called true love.

The river views were incredible with floor-to-ceiling windows in the restaurant and extra-large French balconies in the cabins. With generously sized cabins and two lounges, passengers loved the Captain's Club on the upper deck where the roof slides back to offer a scenic alfresco experience. Free-flowing wine and beer at lunch and dinner, and delicious onboard cuisine added more spice to the trip.

On day five, they set off to see Nuremburg, the second largest city in the federal state of Bavaria. The Kaiserberg Castle was built in 1040 by the German King Henry III, who went on to become The Holy Roman Emperor. The city bears the painful ugly scars of the brutal Nazi regime. Zeppelin Field was the Nazi party's rally ground. After World War II, in 1945-46, the Allied Forces conducted the military tribunals according to International Law, called the Nuremberg trials.

On day six, Jacob and Julie flew into Paris. The Eiffel Tower is a wrought-iron lattice tower on the Champ de Mars in Paris. It was named after the engineer Gustave Eiffel, whose company designed and built the tower. It is a global cultural icon of France and one of the most recognizable structures in the world and the most-visited paid monument in the world. The tower is 1,063 feet tall, about the height of an 81-storey building, and the tallest structure in Paris. The tower has three levels for visitors with restaurants on the first and second levels. The top level's upper platform is 906 feet above the ground.

Day seven was a daytrip to Champagne. Only then Jacob knew that the world-famous drink was named after the region where it was produced. The area is marked by corduroy-shaped vineyards, 125 miles of underground passageways and cellars with a fascinating and intriguing past dating back to Roman times. The giant Reims Cathedral with Mark Chagall stained-glass windows, where most of the French Kings were crowned, towered over all of these. A short walk from there led to Basilica of St Remi, who baptized Clovis, the first king of France in 496 AD.

The guide narrated the history. The underground cellars were used as shelters and schools during world wars. Three varieties of grapes are used in champagne - *pinot noir, pinot meunier and chardonnay*. They went to Epernay, which is the UNESCO World Heritage Centre. The Avenue De Champagne is lined with magnificent champagne houses like Moet & Chandon, Perrier-

Jouet, Martell etc, for half a mile. They indulged in a protracted, pretty posh bar crawl.

Jacob and Julie returned back to their Paris hotel, rested and refuelled. On the night, they went to Moulin Rouge, a cabaret in Paris, which was based on a story about a strange love triangle. A man called Christian befriended Satine, a star courtesan, and fell in love. But the owner of the firm had already promised her to the Duke of Monroth (his potential investor) which caused a tug of war. Its glowing red windmill towering over the Montmartre rooftops was an iconographic representation of French and Parisian culture. They watched the show sitting at one of the candle-lit 'festive tables' and witnessed the archetypal event unfold into reality under their watchful eyes as they sipped premium rosé champagne. The unedifying spectacle was high octane entertainment.

On day eight they flew to Zurich, a global centre for banking and finance in northern Switzerland. The picturesque lanes of the central Altstadt (Old Town), on either side of the Limmat River, reflected its pre-medieval history. Waterfront promenades like the Limmatquai followed the river toward the 17th century Rathaus (town hall). The city was founded by the Romans 2000 years back.

On day nine, they caught the train to Geneva. It is the most populous city of Romandy, the French-speaking part of Switzerland situated where the Rhône exits Lake Geneva. Geneva is a global city, a financial centre and a worldwide centre for diplomacy due to the presence of numerous international organizations including the headquarters of many agencies of the United Nations and the Red Cross. Geneva hosts the highest number of international organizations in the world. The Europe trip came to a grinding halt and on the tenth day they flew back to Manchester. Mark picked them up from the airport.

Mark and Molly arranged a reception for the newlyweds. The wedding reception was usually held after the completion of a marriage ceremony as hospitality for those who have attended the wedding, hence the name 'reception'. Since the wedding was held in Sri Lanka in a hastily arranged setting, most friends and relatives in England could not attend. So, the reception was held for the couple to be received into society for the first time as a married couple in England.

The reception was held at the Gibson Hotel, a wonderful place set in 50 acres of undulating meadow and parkland and boasting a unique 18-hole golf course where once Tiger Woods played. Its hidden escape tunnels lead to the nearby church, dark cellars and a fascinating historic past.

There were 150 guests. The dinner was a sumptuous Indian meal. Mark carefully selected the items to provide the guests' tastebuds with ample variety of authentic Indian cuisine and to create a memorable dining experience. Starters were mixed kebab, samosa and mussels. Main dishes were Tandoori mixed grill, Korai chicken and king prawn Balti. Vegetable dishes were Bombay Aloo, Tarka Dhall and mushroom bhaji. Side dishes composed of Pilaf rice, Peshwari nan and green salad. The atmosphere was relaxed, friendly and full of fun. The Indian dishes retained their identity but had a contemporary twist mirroring the historic culture being given a modern-day makeover by creating individually crafted dishes. There was a selection of desserts - kulfi, Gulab Jamun and Payasam. It was like a warm blanket on a cold winter evening and without a doubt all were craving for the sweet Indian treat.

There was a gigantic multi-layered sandwich cake smiling at the audience. The DJ announced the cake cutting ceremony would be on shortly. Then there was a twist. He surprised everybody saying that 'the bride has been kidnapped.' Mark had secretly arranged for three of his friends dressed in military fatigue to hold Julie and demand a ransom from the groom. The demand had to be 'negotiated' and Jacob had to give two cartons of Carlsberg lager and a bottle of Remy Martin Cognac to release the bride. 'Bride-napping' is a custom in Germany, Romania and some other countries. It was Mark's idea to introduce it in that setting as a surprise.

The bride and groom ceremoniously cut the first piece of cake. As per Roman wedding rite, they fed each other with a slice. Following that, all guests shared the cake.

After that the couple did the 'first dance.' Then it was time for 'dollar dance'; the 'three kidnappers' collected £5 each for those wanting to dance with the bride or groom. The music and dance went on for nearly six hours. The collection reached over £750, which was given to the church as a donation.

A few weeks elapsed. December 1st arrived. For Jacob, there were so many first experiences of Christmas - as a married man, in Europe, away from parents and in his in-laws' house.

A frosted Christmas garland with pinecones and berries was erected on the front door. A seven-foot shimmering mountain fir Christmas tree, well-lit with multi-colour scintillating lights, adorned the living room. Outside was decorated with low-voltage fairy lights, icicles and curtain clusters. The garden was decorated with a galaxy of festoon lights.

The Christmas dinner was very well planned and arranged by Julie. 'Blood Orange Spritz' was her signature cocktail with bubbly citrus topped off with a splash of sparkling wine as the perfect elegant sipper. Mark had ensured Krug Grande Cuvee Champagne was flowing non-stop throughout.

The menu was:
Duck & pork terrine with cranberries & pistachios
Smoked salmon with horseradish crème fraîche & beetroot

Celeriac, hazelnut & truffle soup
Perfect pancetta & roast shallot-stuffed turkey
Brussels sprouts with chestnuts & sage
Roast potatoes
Honey-mustard parsnips
Honey-roast carrots
Spiced red cabbage
Bacon, sausage and prune rolls
Port and cranberry sauce

A classic Christmas pudding with fruity basin served with brandy butter embodied the spirit of Christmas.

After the dinner, it was time for the exchange of Christmas presents. Jacob gave Julie a diamond silver Celtic knot heart pendant necklace. Julie gave Jacob a personalized men's dual leather bracelet.

Jacob and Julie gave Molly a TheraFlow foot massager with dual roller since she used to complain of foot pain. They gave Mark a bottle of Macallan Double Cask Gold Malt whisky and The *Times* newspaper of Mark's date of arrival in the UK prepacked in a sleet black gift box. Mark and Molly gave Jacob a Philips wet and dry men's electric shaver with precision trimmer and gave Julie a MoonLamp based on NASA pictures showing the craters, basins, and mountains of the moon.

Mark's close friend and ex-partner in the legal firm at Edinburgh, had invited all of them for Hogmanay. For Jacob, Hogmanay was a novelty since it is not celebrated on a grand scale in many Asian countries.

They arrived by evening on the 31st of December.

Just before midnight, they all stood up in the living room, in a circle of linked arms which were crossing over one another. At the stroke of twelve announcing the New Year, all started singing 'Auld Lang Syne,' the poem by Robert Burns, and rushed to the centre as a group. Then everybody went out through the kitchen door. Mark had entrusted Jacob do a special task - 'first-footing', the tradition dating back to Viking times, usually by a dark-haired man. Jacob entered first through the front door and gave the Martin family a gift bag containing a bottle of Glenmorangie Signet single malt whisky, shortbread and a rich fruit cake.

There were fireworks to follow. Outside in Edinburgh, 75,000 people were having a six-hour street party. Then they did Ceilidh dancing with music, dancing and storytelling. After that they went to see the Loony Dook, almost a thousand people in ridiculous costumes throwing themselves in the freezing waters of the Firth of Forth.

They all went back to Martin's house, had tea and shortly after set off for home.

6

Gentleman Jim

Mark's best friend was Jim, whom he had known for almost forty years, right from his school days. He was a generous, open-hearted, kind, and indomitable individual. He used to bemoan that gentlemen were steadily declining in numbers almost approaching 'endangered species list,' after Adam was kicked out of the Garden of Eden. Jim was a colonel in the army, a man with succinctly distinguishable characteristics. He did not tolerate any nonsense from anybody and was proud to be a man of principles with an extensive command of English. He was somebody who had his feet firmly planted on the ground. He was a great thinker and philosopher who viewed his work and life through the lens of duty. He always was in a constant quest to reinvent and improve himself. Anybody who came across Jim felt he was genteel with gentleness in him as well as gentlemanliness. He was always cool, calm, and collected. He was a man of astute service, honour and great humour.

Mark considered Jim a loyal friend, a great source of experience and wisdom and an anchor in adversity and adventure. Jim used to say that the good things we do in life go unnoticed and unrewarded. Mark admired the aims and ambitions Jim set for himself because they were based on the virtues he represented. As somebody who has lived with gunfire at close range and lived through the turbulence and turmoil of times, Jim was a seasoned veteran on whom Mark placed his deep trust. Jim lived in a cul-de-sac in the nearby village. As a gentleman, he chose to live far from the madding crowds, out of the prying eyes of the commuter population, avoiding seeing the housing developments which sprout like mushrooms every season. He preferred to live in the vicinity of foxes. His house was away from the noise of trains and buses, which upset his mental equilibrium. He did not put any name board at the gate, since he believed those who wanted to see him already knew where he lived and for those who did not want to see him, he chose to stay out of their reach. Three important people serving him daily were the paper boy, milkman, and the postman.

His natural locomotive was his horse, which was his chosen mode of transport but admitted that due to time constraints, he was forced to use the car many times since punctuality was his priority. His Morris Minor car, sparkling clean, would be parked in his driveway in the take-off position. His dwelling was truly his castle. It was a double-fronted detached bungalow on the edge of a hill. The house comprised of a vestibule, hallway and spacious lounge with a recessed log burner, kitchen, dining room and three well-balanced bedrooms. The garage was detached. His routine was a testament of talent and tenacity. When he described the sufferings of people he came across during his overseas postings, his heart soared and bled for them.

The furniture was handed down through generations – a Victorian era under-stuffed sofa, high-backed chairs and nest of tables. There was a 'snooze-room' with a rocking chair made of oak with two curved bands attached to the bottom of the legs, connecting the legs to each other on one side. The rockers contacted the floor at only two points, giving the occupant the ability to rock back and forth by shifting the weight or pushing lightly with the feet. This was his resting spot with a nightcap after the evening jollifications. The authentically restored and reframed pictures of his ancestors hung on the walls. The relics of his foreign military trips – a Chinese dagger, stuffed Egyptian goose and a twelve-horned antler of Indian swamp deer etc - were on display broadcasting his worldwide travel.

He was a keen gardener. The lush green, well-manicured grass was bordered by shrubs mimicking marching troops. There was a laburnum tree in the front with yellow pea-flowers in pendulous leafless long racemes which made them one of the very popular garden trees. The fruits developed as pods and were extremely poisonous. The yellow flowers were responsible for the old poetic name 'golden chain tree.' Since all parts of the plant were poisonous, Jim put a warning notice on the tree to warn any children passing by. Jim used to tell his visitors that the tree featured in Claude Monet's garden at *Giverny*.

Jacob was still eating with his hands which was socially acceptable back in many Asian countries. Mark thought that he needed to teach him English ways. He phoned Jim and briefed him accordingly and invited him to watch tennis on the TV. Mark called Jacob in to have a chat with Jim and went upstairs to have a shower.

Jim was a man of impeccable manners. His military career as a colonel made him stand out - a class apart from Mark's common friends. Jim started talking about English manners and etiquette. As an introduction to break the ice, Jim recalled his early days in the military. He used to have a colleague, an army major, who was keen on foxhunting.

Jim said, 'One day, while having coffee in the officers' mess, I reminded him of Oscar Wilde's quote on foxhunting "the unspeakable in full pursuit of the uneatable". That shook him up. He gave up foxhunting couple of weeks later.' Jim went on. 'Being a gentleman is a full-time job. One cannot take a day off. One must believe, behave, and act in a club class style throughout. While interacting with public, words coming out of you must be in a measured way, because they count. I believe in being true to who I am. That is how I am able to sleep better knowing I have done the right things.' Jim was a model of punctuality. At functions, he used to comment that only Her Majesty comes *on* time; everybody else must be *in* time.

Jim commented that Edmund Burke remarked, "'A King may make a nobleman, but he cannot make a gentleman". When we go out, ensure that dress is smart with a tie on, hair well- combed, clean fingernails and polished reflective shoes. Whatever has happened that day, one should always put a glow of health and strength on face when interacting with others. Clear and honest dealings pay dividends in life.'

He narrated how he made light work of the various setbacks in life and career and emphasized that one ought to prove the spirit of fight and adopt a never-say-die attitude to overcome unsurmountable odds. He vividly narrated the virtue and vices of life and the hurdles and joys of wedded life. He reiterated that fortitude and forbearance through life's struggles will reap fame and fortune later. Jim pointed out that every day is a boon since we live in the present state, we should set out a viable plan and strategy on a daily basis and expect a moment of magic anytime, which will come unexpected.

Jim promised to take him to a pub to show him around. He explained that a pub or public house was an establishment licensed to serve alcoholic drinks for consumption on the premises. It is open to the public without membership and serves draught beer or cider without requiring food to be consumed. Also, in most pubs, drinks had to be bought at the bar.

Jim went on. 'The pub scene across the world is characterised by its casual warmth and conviviality. It has none of the pretences or formality of a restaurant or cocktail bar. It is the relaxed setting in which friends and strangers alike can choose to meet. The pub is where people go to celebrate special occasions with a group of chums, but also where somebody might go to flirt intimately with a prospective lover. It is a comfortable destination for seeking out the company of others. Most pubs have their own distinct atmosphere and character.

'Pubs are distinguished as much by their interior décor, as by the beer and liquor they sell and the customers that mingle around the bar. These qualities combine to give a 'local' its appeal, with a draw far beyond its immediate locality. These incredibly unique, idiosyncratic attributes of pubs, which were once taken for granted, are now in real danger of extinction, as bar chains with standardised designs and drinks' menus are rolled out across city centres and main streets. Turning its back on the trend towards homogeneity of today's watering holes, the pub scene celebrates the often exuberant, sometimes elegant décor, and always singular, wow factor of public drinking places, whether they are big or small, traditional, or contemporary. If you are not a drinker or are the designated driver, then you can easily order a soft drink. If you are a drinker, then the usual order at a pub consists of lager, ale, bitter and spirits. A request for lager, ale or bitter will usually get you a whole pint unless you specify you want half. It is unlikely pubs will be able to serve you fancy cocktails, for which you would normally go to a bar.'

Jim ordered a three-course meal and demonstrated the usage of cutlery. With the 'European' method, the fork remained in the left hand and the knife helped coax your food onto the fork. The tines remain facing downwards. European style was also referred to as 'hidden handle' because the knife and fork were held in such a way that the handles were tucked into the palm and held by the thumb and forefinger. When finished eating, and to let others know, place knife and folk together, with the prongs (tines) on the fork facing upwards, on the plate.

In the pub, so many people came and greeted Jim. Jacob was inquisitive. Jim remarked 'One should be able to chew the fat with even people with tangential connections in life.'

Jim reminded Jacob about a William of Wykeham quote 'Manners maketh the man.' He reinforced that people should make out one's class by the way he conducts in public. He narrated his profession and ambition with great diligence. He said,

'Broadly speaking, the baggage of negative connotations follows everybody like shadow. You can never win over your shadow; just walk away and it follows you harmlessly.'

Jim always wore a suit which was tailor-made and with a great panache. Noting the bottom button on his suit was unfastened, Jacob enquired why that was left like that. With a sarcastic smile, he replied, 'This goes back to King Edward VII otherwise called "Bertie". He was born in 1841 as the eldest son of Queen Victoria and Prince Albert of Saxe-Coburg and Gotha. He reigned as king from 1901 to 1910. He was known for his extensive dinners and many mistresses. Through most of his childhood, the Queen regnant was the Queen pregnant. Her Majesty had nine children. As Edward grew up, he developed an expanding waistline and was nicknamed "Tum-Tum". He never succeeded to fasten the bottom button of his suit. The gentlemen at that time, followed his style and the tradition has been carried on since then.'

7

Baby Girl

Four months after Jacob's arrival, one morning, while having breakfast, Julie felt light-headed and nauseated. She went up and lay down for an hour or so. Molly went up to the bedroom to check. She was still feeling unwell. Jacob had gone away to attend court in Glasgow for two days. Mark had gone to work. An hour later Julie vomited twice. Molly panicked a bit and phoned Mark. Mark said he would come soon. He came in half an hour. Molly went to have a shower. When Molly came out of the shower, Mark had a beaming smile. Molly felt it a bit strange. Then Mark had to spell it out; Julie was pregnant. Jacob was over the moon. He couldn't rest and in sheer excitement, he told the good news to the partners in his law firm that his fathership was on the way.

She saw the GP, who examined and arranged further check-ups. The midwife took over the care. She was regularly checked on. The midwife noted that Julie was feeling low. She was referred for counselling and the counsellor saw her on a regular basis. Julie slowly lost interest in domestic chores. When Jacob came back from work, he felt Julie had lost interest in him, he couldn't fathom out how depression could affect a family and a sex life.

One of the staff working in his office, Charlotte, dropped in his room and while discussing advice on how to draft a reply in a court case to a client, casually mentioned that she was getting counselling for anxiety and depression and saw Julie coming out after seeing the same counsellor. Jacob didn't quite know exactly how to handle it. Inadvertently, he admitted that Julie was also feeling anxious and depressed. Charlotte was 23 and had been working in the office for a few weeks on a temporary basis. She was five feet four inches tall, with blonde shoulder-length hair, attractive, alluring, dainty and eye-catching. Jacob felt an instant and innocent liking for her not just because she was beautiful but also because she was depressed, like Julie. A few days later, after work, Jacob dropped into Tesco to get some groceries. Coming out, he saw Charlotte waiting at the bus stop. He stopped and offered a lift. She was pleased. While chatting she said that because she is single, she does very little cooking and mainly depends on the microwave for her daily meals. Jacob said he was used to cooking well and promised to show her his skills in cooking Sri Lankan dishes.

The next day, a few minutes after Jacob came to work, there was a knock on his door and Charlotte walked in with a radiant smile and a cup of coffee. She put it on his desk and said,

'Thanks a lot for yesterday; it was very kind of you.' Jacob felt some psychic coincidence since he was about to ask for coffee anyway. Feeling romantic love running along certain chemical pathways through the brain which were triggered instantly, she stood still with a radiant smile.

Jacob replied, 'No problem. That is my usual route. If you need anything, let me know. By the way, are you feeling better after seeing the counsellor? Julie has only started seeing him a couple of weeks back. Is he good?'

'Yes and no. Can I talk to you some other time? I have an urgent letter to dispatch.' She turned around, took about four steps, paused, turned her head back and waved with a radiant smile and said, 'Have a good day.'

Jacob had a sip of the coffee, got up suddenly and looked in the mirror, stroked his wavy hair and sat down. He licked his lips with a gratifying and engrossing feeling of elation which went from his head to his toes. He twisted his lips into a smirk.

Back at home, Julie's vomiting, called hyperemesis in pregnancy, got worse. Also she was still feeling low, lethargic and disinterested. Jacob was feeling rejected. He tried to encourage her by praising and helping her with daily chores. There was an increasing lack of warmth between them. Their ways travelled parallel like a railway track.

Three weeks later, one of the staff dropped in with a card for Jacob to sign, since Charlotte's temporary job would be finishing the next day. Jacob made a broad enquiry about what they were going to get her. The reply was, 'I know she likes pink gin and red wine; we might get any of them.' He duly signed it and gave a £5 contribution towards her leaving gift. Jacob felt a sharp and sudden sense of loss. He leaned back on the chair, gazed through the window and saw a skylark singing and going uphill to the sky and all of a sudden plummeted back to earth. He felt restless and uncomfortable the whole day. He thought, I must not let emotions take over me; it will affect my standing in the firm.

The next day, Friday, Julie was very unwell with tummy pain, vomiting and rigors. So Jacob took the day off and rang the GP. He visited her at home. She had a urinary infection and was started on antibiotics.

On Monday, when Jacob went to work, he noted a sealed envelope marked 'Private and Confidential' on his desk. He opened it hastily. It read: 'I couldn't say bye to you since you were not in the office today. I wish you all the best.' Charlotte (mobile number). Jacob texted her by 11am. 'I am sorry to hear you have left. If you are in, can I drop in at 5.30 today?' She texted back quickly, 'Yes, I will be in.' At lunchtime, Jacob went to Tesco and bought some gifts.

A sense of immense anticipation bubbled within Charlotte. By twenty past five, she was ready, pulled the chair towards the window and sat waiting, peering out through the net curtains. Jacob arrived at 5.30, right on time. Before he could press the doorbell, Charlotte eagerly opened the door. She was wearing a knee-length apricot long sleeve bodycon, which embraced her tightly, explicitly, and elicited her excellent body contours and curves. The golden long hair with bushy curls were flowing over her shoulders and scattered over her bosoms. Her rose-gold lace chain broad choker necklace radiated a unique sense of attraction. Light pink lipstick matched the rouge on her cheeks.

As soon as Jacob walked in, Charlotte greeted him with a kiss on the cheek and embraced him saying, 'Thanks for dropping in.' There was an instant and spontaneous gushy rush of affection and warmth between them. They stood in an embrace for a few seconds in silence in front of the long mirror at the entrance, while Jacob got lost in the appreciation of the reflection of her pristine physique.

Releasing the embrace, Jacob gave her a bunch of variegated tulips. Charlotte's eyes lit up. She wasn't sure of the meaning of variegation. She threw it at Jacob's face what it meant. With an affectionate smile he said, 'This means beautiful eyes.' When she blushed, her lips appeared full and soft.

Charlotte asked him to sit down. He sat on the settee. She sat beside him and when she pushed the obstructing hair sideways, her dangling Dior-white crystal Claire D Lune palladium stud earrings sparkled. Jacob gave her a bottle of Chateau Pontet-Canet red wine.

She just screamed in sheer delight, 'Wow.' The exclamation was marked with such an accent of passion. Jacob sat still watching her through the corners of his eyes with a subtle and sublime smile.

'Amazing; this is my favourite wine; how did you know?'
'It is telepathy.'

'Thanks a lot for the gifts and your kindness.'
'What can I get you to drink?'
'A cup of tea will do.'

Jacob scanned the sitting-come-dining room. It was small with a settee, two chairs, a sideboard and dining table with four chairs. The wall paper was fine decor marblesque fractal rose gold metallic.

Sipping the tea, Jacob enquired, 'Is this Ceylon Tea?'
'Yes.'
'How did you know that this is my favourite?'
'Oh, it is also telepathy.'

She burst into a bout of chuckle gleefully in rollicking exuberance. Her voice reverberated criss-cross across the walls in vibrant, vivid and vociferous notes like the trills and chortles of a kookaburra.

Jacob enquired, 'Have you got any jobs lined up?'
'Sort of, I have a friend who has two horses. She needs them looking after since she has some knee problems. It is only for a couple of months. After that I don't know.' She remained mute after that.

'So, you like horse riding?'
'Yes, I love it; I used do a lot of horse riding.'
'I have never rode a horse.'
'I will teach you that; no problem.'

Jacob slipped into a pensive mood.

Charlotte interrupted with a tinge of curiosity, 'Have you got a long name?,
'My full name is Jacob De Silva. Why did you ask that?'
'I have been intrigued by your ex cricket captain's name.'
'Who?'
'Denagamage Proboth Mahela De Silva Jayawardene; I thought you were related.'

Jacob chuckled and quipped, 'Our previous captain carries my surname but he is no relation of mine.'

'The fast bowler also has a very long name; Warnakulasurya Patabendige Ushantha Joseph Chaminda Vaas.'

They both laughed loudly.

Charlotte enquired, 'Can you tell me more about Sri Lanka?'

'The country was called Ceylon. It was British Colony from 1815 to 1948.'

Charlotte prompted 'Shall we make a deal? You teach me Sri Lankan cooking; I will teach you horse riding. Agreed?' She offered her outstretched palm.

Jacob gently squeezed her palm with both hands and peered deep into her blue eyes and murmured with glee, 'Ya, deal agreed.' He went on. 'Please let me know how you get on with things. If there is anything you need, please don't hesitate to contact me. You can text me any time. It is lovely to have worked with you.' Jacob got up.

Charlotte also got up. 'I don't know what to say; you are a very kind person. Once I started getting to know you, I had to leave since I lost my job.'

'Sorry, I have to make a move now. I will be in touch.'

Charlotte gave him a kiss on the other cheek and Jacob left saying 'bye.'

When Jacob left, she ran both hands through the hair, shook her head back and forth twice so that her hair could get the freedom and air and slumped on the settee, with a feeling of pleasure and an ache of loss. She got lost in thought and woke up when the clock chimed seven times.

When Jacob got home, Molly, Mark and Julie were already waiting with dinner ready on the table. Jacob went straight to the dinner table. Julie noticed a lipstick mark on his cheek and after passing a glance at Molly, quipped,

'You are late today, was there any problem?' She looked flushed and with blazing eyes passed a quick glare at Jacob.

Clearing his throat, Jacob replied, 'Sort of.'

There was a weird mute feeling on the dining table.

Halfway through the dinner, Julie burst into tears, got up, pushed the chair backwards and left like a guided missile slamming the door and thumping up the steps shaking the house sending an ominous threat to all. Jacob instantly followed her up to the bedroom.

Mark and Molly stared speechlessly at each other.

In a couple of minutes, there was an almighty row between Julie and Jacob.

Julie shouted, 'If you want another woman, so be it; I've had enough.'

'Sorry. Let me explain.'

'What is there to explain? Another pack of lies?'

Jacob remained quiet to dampen the temperature. He left saying, 'I will talk to you later,' allowing her time to cool down.

Mark also didn't finish his dinner. He started pacing up and down in front of the fireplace. When Jacob came down, Mark grinned and said with a sceptical lifting of the eyebrows,

'Can you just have a look in the mirror?

Jacob went to the cloakroom and to his horror, Charlotte's parting kiss had left a calling card on his cheek. Although he tried to rub it off, it wouldn't vanish. He had to indulge in washing with soap and water twice before the reluctant flame of his romantic encounter finally got extinguished. He knew he was caught rather red-handed. He did not have a leg to stand on. He stayed downstairs watching TV for the rest of the night to avoid pandemonium.

Molly went up to Julie on a peace mission. Julie was still in a foul mood. She dispatched her instantly.

'Mum, it has nothing to do with you.'

Molly left gently closing the door.

The next day, Jacob got up early and set off for work. He called Julie to say 'bye'. She just pulled the quilt cover over her head, turned way and stayed in bed with a deadly silence. Jacob made a calculated, unceremonious exit.

The marriage which began with passion, conviction and devotion, was indeed turning prematurely frosty and rusty. A state of peace and tranquility was slipping into a phase of mistrust, tension and bickering. Even trivial things started getting on Julie's nerves. One day, Jacob, was rushing off to work in the morning and left plates in the sink after breakfast. Julie made an issue out of that. She felt like giving him a stern telling- off but she bit her tongue and bottled up the frustration. Jacob started getting more self-conscious and felt rejected. He felt that blood was thicker than water and it was a three against one tug of war in the household. He started feeling exploited just as a pay cheque. Although four people were living under the same roof, all the food and drinks were bought by Jacob. Jacob felt Molly and Julie had teamed up in this raw deal. He found it difficult and incapable of putting this issue on the table and have a meaningful and rational way to resolve. Also, Julie would go out on her own some days, presumably to the post office or bank but didn't always tell Jacob what she did or where she went. One day, when Jacob asked her at dinner,

'Did you go out today?'

She snapped instantly, 'Why? Are you checking on me?'

The mutual ambivalence slowly replaced the cheerful household into a state of suffocating stillness, frustration, and unhappiness. Bickering went on even in the darkness of the bedroom, interrupting the proceedings. Jacob could not put up with this and found temporary reprieve by going down to the living room and watching TV or movies, lying on the settee with a quilt and some pillows and slowly slipping into sleep there. Jacob felt like a boarder and lodger in the in-laws' mansion. Nearly a fortnight passed after the quarrel in the frosty and suspicious environment.

One day, after breakfast, Mark was in the lounge reading a newspaper. Julie enquired whether he wanted tea. He said 'yes'. When Julie came with the tea, he asked her to sit down.

In a friendly, fatherly and philosophical tone, he started, 'Trust in an intimate relationship is rooted in feeling safe with another person. Infidelity, lies or broken promises can severely damage the trust between a husband and wife. That, however, does not necessarily mean that a marriage can't be salvaged. Although rebuilding trust can be challenging when there is a significant breach, it is, in fact, possible if both partners are committed to the processes.'

Julie started thinking. The fundamental tenet in marriage is trust.

Mark continued, 'It takes much time and effort to re-establish the sense of safety you need for a marriage to thrive and continue to grow. Recovery from the trauma caused by a break in the trust is where many couples who want to get back on track can get stuck.'

Julie nodded in partial approval. In her head, questions were teeming. She felt she acted subconsciously without really trying to find out and understand what happened. The bitterness and resentment to Jacob were still leaving a bad taste in her mouth. She leaned back on the settee, with clenched fists and half-closed eyes as though in meditation. Although she thought she knew Jacob inside out, she could not figure out his movements. Her heart was searing and burning with a myriad of suspicion, jealousy, and hate.

Feeling her indecisive state, after a short pause of repose, Mark just prompted, 'Have a rest and think over what I said.'

Julie went up to her bedroom, tried to bring her wandering mind back in line. Her senses were swimming after the quarrel. She put out some clothes for washing, went outside and sat on the steps facing the back garden, in deep solitude, to clear her head and regain her mental equilibrium.

When Molly returned from the church, Mark was still reading his newspaper. They held a politburo meeting with a view to mediate. But both felt it would be better that a neutral person outside the household would be the best option and decided to persuade the warring couple to see a marriage counsellor.

At work, Jacob couldn't concentrate. He started fidgeting, drinking coffee, cup after cup, and pondering and gazing. He felt foggy, bleary-eyed and yawned excessively. He asked the secretary to come in. He enquired what urgent work was due. She said there was a court report to be sent by the next day.

He said, 'Can you bring it through? I will try to do it. Meanwhile can you prepare a list of jobs to be done over the next two weeks?'

Mark felt being drawn into a whirlpool of conflicts and comforts in a confetti. He didn't have anyone to turn to. He thought over the options whether to get professional counselling regarding marital issues. Thinking it over, he thought he would get some books to start with. At lunchtime, he went to the council library and got three books. In the introductory chapter, he read, 'Make note of it, acknowledge it, and put it in a mental parking lot to think about later, when you can discuss it with someone else, or when you are not at work and have lots to do.'

He started writing down the action plan: (a) cut down distractions in the average workday. When big things are happening outside of the office, whether they are good or bad, it becomes increasingly difficult to tackle the work because emotional state is directly tied to the level of focus. (b) Avoid viewing negative news because one is likely to see his own personal worries as more threatening and severe. (c) Avoid multitasking since it sabotages productivity. (d) Make a list of your top three priorities for that day; that short list will keep you focused on the bigger picture. (e) Stop Fidgeting and Start Focusing. As advised in the book, after working an hour, Jacob went out for walk for ten minutes to have a complete break and get some fresh air.

Two days later, Mark took the whole family to the Sharmila Indian Restaurant for a meal. Things were spoken generally on a low key. Mark put the idea of seeing a marriage counsellor. After a heavy pause, Jacob nodded in approval. Julie followed suit by saying she would agree to that.

The next week, Jacob and Julie went to see a reputable private counsellor. After his introduction, he emphasized,

'Whether you were the offending partner or the betrayed, to rebuild the trust in your marriage, both of you must renew your commitment to your marriage and to one another.'

He gave them both written action plans as described in the book *Contemporary Family Therapy* by Winek & Craven and requested them to work on the following regime:

Know the Details - The offending partner should be upfront and honest with information, in addition to giving clear answers to any and all questions from their partner. This will give the betrayed party a broader understanding of the situation.

Release the Anger - Even minor breaches of trust can lead to mental, emotional, and physical health problems. Make the partner aware of all these feelings.

Show Commitment - Both parties, especially the betrayed, may be questioning their commitment to the relationship and wondering if the relationship is still right for them or even salvageable.

Acts of empathy - Sharing pain, frustration, and anger; showing remorse and regret; and allowing space for the acknowledgment and validation of hurt feeling can be healing to both parties.

Building off this, defining what both sides require from the relationship can help give partners the understanding that proceeding the relationship comes with clear expectations that each person, in moving ahead, has agreed to fulfil. Both parties must work to define what is required to stay committed to making the relationship work.

Rebuilding Trust - Together, both partners must set specific goals and realistic timelines for getting the marriage back on track. Decide to forgive or to be forgiven.

Be open to self-growth and improvement - The underlying causes for the betrayal need to be identified, examined and worked on by both spouses for the issues to stay dormant.

Be aware of your innermost feelings and share your thoughts - Leaving one side to obsess about the situation or action that broke the trust is not going to solve anything. Instead, it is important to openly discuss the details and express all feelings of anger and hurt.

Once the above points have been taken to heart by both sides, talk openly about the goals and check regularly to make sure both are on track.

Take responsibility for own actions and decisions; apologize for the hurt caused and avoid defensiveness, which will only perpetuate the conflict. Justifying your behaviour based on what your spouse is doing or has done in the past is also not productive.

Work on understanding why and what went awry in the relationship before the betrayal actually took place. While this won't help to forget what happened, it may help to get some answers to move on.

Provide positive responses and reinforcement to help give the partner consistent feedback to things that please once committed to giving partner a second chance.

While there's independent work to do, remember to listen completely to one another. Remind one another that each deserves open and honest answers to questions about the betrayal.

Rebuilding the Relationship - Both must work on treating the relationship like it is a completely new one. Both sides must ask for what they really need and not expect their partner to simply know what it is they want. In rebuilding a mutually supportive connection, come to an agreement about what a healthy relationship looks like to both.

There were six counselling sessions on a weekly basis. Both Jacob and Julie felt they were benefitting and things were slowly getting back to near normal. Julie had episodes of lethargy which were out of the blue. The GP found that she had developed gestational diabetes which compounded her problems.

In Julie's mind, there were still nagging doubts about Jacob, although she did not let it override her emotional status quo. The anger had dissipated and she could analyze things in a rational and cool manner. She felt she should give him the benefit of doubt and re-establish trust.

Mark and Molly felt that they needed to clear the whole air in the household. So, they arranged a Chinese takeaway one evening to ease the burden of cooking and have time off from the culinary department. They knew well that they had experienced their own heavy shares of sadness, strife and sorrows in the past. They all ate the meal. Eating at home was much more comfortable than in a restaurant, in more comfortable casual clothes, in a comfortable position on favourite chairs. At home there was no worry about disturbing other diners and they could talk and laugh as loudly as they wished without fear of upsetting people sitting nearby tables.

Mark made the mission statement while having coffee after the meal. Jacob's face was a bit tensed up with anticipation of fear of any further confession or concession, and he strove to dispel even the very thought of it. He was weighed down with the harsh reality of his weakness face to face with necessity to get on with life. Julie decided to throw down the glove of challenge. Hatred had fled from her heart. She decided to shake impressions which had become suffocating and unbearable.

Mark used his subtle skills and diplomacy. He opened up. 'Since you have both had counselling over the last couple of months and sorted out things with professional help, I am not going into that territory.' He emphasized the reconciliation and they all stood up and said the Lord's prayer. Then Mark asked all to sit down.

He read the passages from the Bible, which were carefully earmarked by Molly. 'Leave your gift there in front of the altar. First go and be reconciled to them; then come and offer your gift.'
- Matthew 5:24

'Bear with each other and forgive one another if any of you has a grievance against someone. Forgive as the Lord forgave you.'
- Colossians 3:13

Julie's eyes darted from side to side. She moistened her lips and swallowed hard and listened with avidity. Jacob remained rather mute and attentive to every syllable he was hearing, like a school boy listening to a Sunday School teacher. He sat resting his elbows on his knees and gripping his head between his hands.

Back in the office, work was getting better. Jacob won a difficult case in court for a client who had moved in from a different legal firm. That was well appreciated by the partners in the firm. Jacob continued the very early start to the workday, being the first to arrive in the office in the morning. The main reason for that was that he felt more productive when the office was not officially open for the day. That meant there were no phone calls, client meetings, or court appearances so that he could focus on the other tasks on the to-do list.

Jacob took on some additional responsibilities which were: interpreting laws and applying them to specific cases, gathering evidence for a case and researching public and other legal records, examining legal data to determine advisability of defending or prosecuting lawsuit, preparing and drafting legal documents eg legal briefs, wills, deeds, mortgages, leases etc, negotiating settlements and supervising legal assistants.

Jacob started enjoying his newly added responsibilities and enrichment by pay rise. He had turned a new corner; there were plenty of opportunities of furthering his career ahead.

Three months elapsed. It was a Friday afternoon about 4. Jacob got a text from Charlotte 'Can you ring me when you a get chance, please?' Jacob rang in ten minutes.

Charlotte gave an apologetic request. 'Sorry, I didn't mean to disturb you at work; I wanted to discuss something personal. Would it be OK to meet up at the Tesco car park this evening when you finish work?'

He pondered for a few seconds and said, 'I finish at 5. I think 5.30 should be OK. I will park at the far corner near the filling station.'

'OK, Thanks a lot.'

Jacob reached the car park by 5.20. He started feeling a sense of immense anticipation compounded by surprise of sensual sweetness of surprise What is it about?

Charlotte arrived duly on time. Jacob opened the passenger side door for her. She was wearing a lemon one-shoulder fluted hem lace dress with matching yellow Dunhu elegant pretty little young lady's pumps.

Jacob sat with a welcoming fixed smile and a smooth glance. She sat on the front seat and when eagerly turned her left shoulder, the other shoulder hinged towards the seat. She appeared sleek and smooth like silk, impregnated with impeccable manners.

She opened up. 'Sorry to drag you in at short notice. I have some news; I have been selected for the Burghley horse trial in Stamford. It is in three weeks' time. Zara Phillips, Olympian and equestrian will be there for the valedictory function.' She said it all in one breath like a rehearsed speech.

Jacob shrugged his shoulders off-handedly and with a sanguine expression said, 'Wow that is great news.'

She bit her lip and leaned forward, placed her hand softly like a feather on Jacob's wrist almost encircling his watch, peered into his eyes with pleading look and said, 'I would very much like to invite you for this.' There was a shrewd glint in her blue eyes which bewitched him a couple of times.

For a moment, he appeared nervous and paralyzed into inaction and sighed. His eyes narrowed into slits and observed every flicker of movements on her sculpted face.

'Please think it over. Can I let you know by tomorrow?'

'OK. Do you think it is a possibility?' She said slowly, her face turning pale and soft.

'Affirmative.'

A smile began in her eyes, and slowly spread to the lips and corners of her mouth. As the smile broadened, two large dimples appeared on the cheeks. The moments were mesmerizing and conquering which prompted Jacob to whisper,

'Listen, I will let you know by 10 tonight.' Charlotte left soon.

Getting home, Jacob felt restless. He started pacing up and

down. He thought it is best to go for a walk so he could think things over with a clear mind. He went to the park which had lots of trees and shrubs all around it as well as some amazing flowers which had really strong, vibrant colours and incredible smells.

Jacob sat on a bench in a remote corner, took a notepad and started writing his thoughts and action plan. First and foremost- should I go or should I not? No lady has ever invited me in my life in such a way; it was coming freely from her heart. She is of course beautiful; but more than that, she has a wonderful personality. She has broken all my defences and got into me in such a short time. If I go, that will make her a very happy person. If I don't, she would feel rejected or fall out with me. I'd better go.

Should I tell Julie the truth? It will probably be the end of the marriage. It will upset my family and Julie's family. Also, it can affect my standing in the firm at work. Julie is not well in herself. Her mother had miscarried. If this causes emotional upset which is likely, it may trigger a miscarriage and will be a big black mark on me. So, telling Julie is not a viable option. Moreover, Julie has not been keen on me for a while. She has been very cross and continues to be hostile. I need some solace and comfort. What should I tell Julie? Anyway, I go for conferences once a month. I could tell her that I am going for one.

Jacob made up his mind. He told Julie at dinnertime that he would be away for a couple of days on a conference, three weeks later. She didn't seem to be bothered or she didn't mind either way.

Jacob texted Charlotte about 10 at night to say that he would come. She texted back, *A big Thank You!* xx

Three weeks later, Charlotte left with the horse in the van. Jacob followed her in his car. She had arranged a comfortable seat for Jacob. He got some information leaflets on equestrianism. He watched keenly and videoed the various items. The reining or dressage - the riders guided horses through a precise pattern of circles, spins, and stops. In this horseback riding style, work is done at a lope or a gallop. The horse was controlled with little or no apparent resistance. Gymkhana was timed obstacle riding on horseback with a variety of different individual and team events which displayed the speed, agility, control, and responsiveness of the horse. A saddle seat competition was designed to show off the high trotting tendencies of breeds such as the American Saddlebred, Morgan and Arabian. The horse was judged on its elegant movement at a walk, trot, and canter.

Charlotte came first in two formats. She was awarded the winning medals.

Jacob had taken a room at the Mayfield Manor House Hotel, which was located in the nearby picturesque landscape. He drove under an archway into a long yard, at the further end of which were the stables and coach houses. The hotel was full-on gothic style, representing dark medievalism with turrets and gargoyles. The walls were panelled in oak, with a lofty carved arched ceiling.

The room was plush and inviting with a full length mirror with lighting, blackout shades, flat screen TV, stocked mini bar, wifi, newspapers, electric safe and laundry bags. The kingsize bed with memory foam mattress was covered with an Apricity pink velvet bedspread, digital flower print pillows and wide knit lilac blush throws. The wardrobe appeared polished to perfection. The en-suite bathroom contained bathrobes, slippers, large fluffy towels, luxury toiletries and spa treatments. There was a collection of variegated fresh roses on the table emitting a delicate scent.

Jacob picked her up after the trials and went to the room. Giving her time and space to have shower and get changed, he said he would wait at the hotel lobby.

Charlotte had a nice refreshing shower and got dressed up for the dinner. She wore a Cheongsam young lady red sequin off-shoulder elegant mesh dress maxi gown, Amy Q sexy women's satin high heel sandals, an elegant Cambric fascinator party hat and short satin red style gloves. She put on a pink tourmaline CZ silver necklace with a matching luxury long big pink tourmaline CZ silver pendant. She had a purple clutch purse chain handbag. She put on the perfume Olympea by Paco Rabanne. Confidence, certainty and power radiated from the fresh, oriental perfume. The combination of sensual salty vanilla mixed in the aquatic essence was so incredibly uplifting and refreshing.

Forty minutes later, when she was ready, she rang Jacob. When Jacob came in, he felt a bit out of sorts; for a moment he thought he had gone into the wrong room or was visualizing a totally strange lady. He couldn't believe his eyes; he stood still, staring and dazed at the living object of sensual beauty.

They gently strolled to the dining room. There were 36 guests. The subdued lighting set the mood to start a perfect meal. There was a low level of background music, whilst still being able to hear. When they approached the restaurant, there was an aura of chit-chat intermingled with the sporadic clink of glasses. The dining room was exquisite. The walls were covered with a shimmering gold paper and in the middle of the ceiling above the carved oak table was a candelabra. Down the centre of the table was a runner with a Celtic design woven in gold and green into the fabric itself. At the end of the table were floor to ceiling French doors, left slightly ajar to let in the scented summer air. The polished silver cutlery was heavy to the hand and shone brightly in the early evening light. At each place stood a tall empty wine glass and there were beautifully folded napkins to match the runner. The way catering staff were serving bore testament to their experience and ebullience.

Soon after sitting down, the waitress, an attractive red-cheeked, blue-eyed busty lady in her twenties approached them to take the order. She appeared sandy-haired with a soft, selective and seditious smile. Her eyes were glinting with glee at as she approached Jacob. Charlotte noted that Jacob's gaze had landed on her breasts. She squeezed his hand until the knuckles squeaked, a timely reminder to Jacob.

There was a generous supply of Moet and Chandon Champagne served in flutes as frequently as needed. The six-course dinner menu included chilli lime baked shrimp cups as hors d'oeuvre, broccoli leek soup, smoked salmon appetizer bites, pork chops with fig and grape Agro dolce as main course, salad, chocolate and honeycomb ice cream terrine recipe and coffee and tea. The sumptuous meal in the elegant restaurant embraced the expectations of Charlotte.

After dinner, they slipped into the bar, had two helpings of a 'Boomerang' cocktail. Jacob wanted to go to the loo. Charlotte said she would go to the room. She went to the room and got changed into a lace slit V-neck nightie and waited impatiently.

As Jacob walked in, he got stung straightaway for the second time by the strikingly stunning beauty in front of him. He was suddenly being sucked in and seduced succinctly by a modern-day Cleopatra. He felt that her beauty had been unknown, unspoken and unexpressed in the realms of real life.

The slender waist, whistling down from her bust, as smoothly as the water from a waterfall, the curve of her midriff, so voluptuous that Jacob felt as if she was sculpted out by Michael Angelo. The bends of her hips and the fullness of her bosom reminded him of the perfect frame of Venus. The glistening skin strikingly complemented in contrast the redness of her nightwear. As she was caressing her hair with those long slender arms, her navel was naked for the world to view and the prominent carves of her body revealed by the transparent dress caused Jacob's heart to skip a few beats. The broad and expressive eyes gazing atop the amazing narrow glossy swan neck, made the focal point of attraction. Jacob paused, pondered, smiled and gazed. He felt an instantaneous and intriguing infatuation.

Charlotte greeted him with a gentle head-butt, winked playfully and prompted, 'Sit down and close your eyes please.' Glowing with proprietorial pride she put a Defang necktie handkerchief, silk paisley floral tie and pocket square cufflink set in his hands and said, 'Now you can open your eyes.' Jacob was gobsmacked and in a sudden frenzy of emotional commotion and unprecedented rush of extreme surge in adrenaline, he lifted her and threw her up only to support her back in mid-flight on the way down.

They took red wine from the minibar and started sipping slowly enjoying every miniscule of a drop. They sat on the settee.

Jacob said, 'Can I see your hand please?'

With natural curiosity, she stretched and placed her hand in his palm. Jacob commented gleefully, 'The Mount of Venus is located on the palm of the hand at its base, between the thumb and the lifeline. It is an indicator of love, romance, passion, sensuality, the lovers one chooses and physical appearance. This mount is elevated, which means that you are an attractive and healthy individual who is passionate about the arts and the finer things in life. This represents that you are respected, influential and enjoy the benefits of true friendship.' While he described Venus, the Roman Goddess of beauty, she was filled with excitement.

Charlotte went to the toilet. On the way back, her mobile phone accidentally slipped out and she bent down to pick it up. The nightie slipped away displaying her heart-shaped Kim Kardashian-style butt. Her prying eyes caught him with his gaze fixed at her butt. To avoid embarrassment, he commented,

'The female butt is the place where the male eyesight gets stuck on because of the animal instinct. After all we are also just animals in a bit smarter and shy manner. Though we are civilized, it won't ever be enough to completely remove that animal instinct from human nature.'

Impressed with his candid expression and sense of humour, she laughed loud, bright and cheerful like dandelions in summer days blossoming on the field, with radiating dimples and the ripples filling the bedroom.

Jacob started showing her the video clips of the horse trial. She sat down watching, giggling and screaming with joy at times. She went to the bathroom and returned in a few minutes. Her eyes were sparkling with passion and excited with high voltage. She marched towards Jacob and pinched the phone.

'No need to see the video now; you can see the real one,' she said with a wink and sweet and sour smirk.

She perched onto his torso, and Jacob was knocked back on the settee due to the thrust. He barely had a glimpse of only her chin and the choker necklace, the view being obstructed by the pair of throbbing mounts of her craving breasts in his eyeline. So potent was her sexual appeal that he felt dizzy, inexperienced, and breathless with immense excitement and anticipation, in her arms. She pulled him towards her with fierce force and squeezed tight that his ribs creaked. Before Jacob could say anything, the words were lost against her persistent passionate pouting lips which were blossom-like. He caged her in his arms and rolled over on the settee.

About half an hour later, they moved onto the kingsize bed, both sipping champagne. Charlotte slowly undressed. Jacob yelped at being caught when she saw him staring at her out of astonishment of witnessing the ultimate creation of God's beauty in such a close-up. A megawatt current jolted his heart. When she broke into smile, her beguiling, oyster-white teeth sparkled in the muffled lights. Her sculpted figure was twine-thin. The glossy skin was so smooth and reflective. The long hair tumbled over her shoulders. The strawberry-red lips were blossoming. The pencil-thin eyebrows eased down gently to her black, beetle's-leg velvety eyelashes.

Filed to perfection, her red fingernails ran through the hair with spools of it plunging around her photogenic face. The elegant and smooth swan neck was flashing in between. The blue eyes were sparkling like jewels melted on to snow. The dainty nose was surrounded by rosy cheeks and the ears were like those of a sea-nymph.

The decanter-shaped wasp-waist danced in tune competing with each other when she walked, revealing magnetic sex appeal. Like the sculpted hindquarters of a marble statue, like binary crescent moons, the heart-shaped butt gave a scintillating and breath-taking spectacle and he found hard to take his eyes off her. The dimples of Venus were eye-catching, seductive and were giving Jacob secretly coded messages of impending sex.

She whispered to him in a dulcet voice as sweet as a songbird. When she kissed Jacob, he went into a frenzy of passion and the pink lips tasted like rose petals. The scaphoid belly was decorated with a rotund, ostensible, sparkling, and mysterious navel. Jacob was flabbergasted by her fleshy, curved, sensuous, lovely voluptuous and maddening thighs.

Jacob sighed in disbelief, 'My mistress is a dream girl.'

They had a wonderful time until three in the morning, when they dosed off in sheer exhaustion. They got up at 8.30, got ready and had breakfast. Shortly after, they set off separately back home.

Jacob arrived at Charlotte's flat sharply at 5.30. Charlotte saw him through the window and opened the door before he could press the doorbell.

***

Julie gave birth to a bouncing baby girl, weighing seven pounds and two ounces on Sunday morning at 4.20. The baby was cute. The newborn cries filled the room and Jacob burst into tears of relief and joy. He turned his glossy eyes to Julie and in the most tender and soft tone, murmured that they have a beautiful daughter. Although exhausted, she smiled and scanned her eyes to welcome the baby brought to lie on her bare skin. She shed the sweetest tears she has ever done. All the pain of the hard labour melted away like snow under a warm sun.

A new occupant joined the house. Cute cries echoed within the four walls spilling infectious joy and excitement to all. The baby smile was as sweet as a summer strawberry and filled all with a new lasting shine and fervour. The household went into a frenzy of celebration. Mark and Molly accepted their grandparent status by thanking God and embracing each other.

Jacob went on a shopping spree. Although he knew it was a baby girl, he was superstitious that if he had bought things in advance, things might go wrong. So, he had to do all the shopping for the baby in a hurry. He bought a pink mum and baby luxury gift hamper which contained bibs, burp clothes, a breast pump, milk storage containers, nursing bras, breast pads and lotion for sore nipples.

The christening was organized in two weeks. The christening ceremony was the formal welcoming of a new baby into the religious community in which the child was born. It was held in the church. Fr Thomas welcomed the family and members of the congregation participating in the christening ceremony by being in the audience. He mentioned the reason all had come together was to christen the baby and welcome her into the church community.

He asked the parents to come forward and step up to the altar where the christening would take place. Julie held the baby so that she was lying in her arms with her head toward the priest. He read a Bible verse pertaining to being christened. He asked the parents to state their dedication and agreement to their commitment for raising the child with the teachings of the Catholic Church. He obtained commitment from the godparents also to commit to helping to raise the child under the faith of the parents. The priest anointed using a small water pitcher and basin to pour the holy water over the child's head. She was named Paige. Once the baby was christened, she became officially part of the church community. The priest announced it and welcomed the baby into the community.

A new baby brought new problems. Julie was breastfeeding. Since the baby cried as and when, although she was fed, she wasn't sure what the problem was. When the health visitor came, she discussed this with her. The health visitor was well-experienced. She explained,

'Most babies cry a lot until about four months old. They cry if they are hungry, sleepy, uncomfortable, wet nappies or bloated. Crying is worse in late afternoons.' She went on. 'Each baby is unique. You will slowly pick up what the baby wants by the tone of the cry.'

Julie enquired, 'What do I do if she cries a lot?'

'A crying baby is trying to win your heart. Each time a baby cries you give a loving response, she is interacting and building a closer relationship with you.'

'Is it OK to take her out when she is crying?'

'The rhythm of walking probably reminds the baby of when she was in the womb. Movements in general and a drive in the car can be soothing and settling for the baby.'

Julie found it tiring to feed her at night so she slept with the baby. Jacob started sleeping downstairs on the settee after watching TV late into the night. Slowly and steadily, an emotional gap appeared between Julie and Jacob which widened as the weeks flew past. Frustration slowly crept in.

Jacob started comfort eating and drinking three to four glasses of wine at night to relax and sleep. He slowly put on weight. Despite the new baby, he felt lonely and rejected coming home.

One day, Molly got a call from Melbourne. Her uncle Frazer had been taken ill and hospitalized. He'd had a heart attack. He was 68 and a widower, without any children. He was immensely rich and had a kangaroo farm. Molly decided to visit him. She left in a week. Frazer had been discharged from hospital by then. He lived in a brick two-storey house with four bedrooms and a tiled roof.

In addition to a laundry, kitchen, dining and lounge room, most have 3–4 bedrooms and 1 or 2 bathrooms. They generally include a car port or garage. In the more up-market homes, there will also be a separate living area and the main bedroom will have an en-suite bathroom (the second bathroom), and walk-in robe. The other bedrooms may have a built-in wardrobe. The main bathroom and toilet are usually separate rooms.

Frazer's neighbour had arranged a home help in the form of Andrea, a 23-year-old Romanian lady. Molly took an instant dislike to her, triggered by suspicion and jealousy. She assured her uncle that she would stay for three weeks and in the meantime would find a Sri Lankan home help. Frazer started mobilizing gradually. He had been advised to do a one-mile walk daily. Molly took him for walks with religious precision. She started talking about plans for future care. She got rid of Andrea, telling her she would send for her when needed.

Molly established a routine. She would make porridge for breakfast and sandwiches for lunch. Tea was always with a couple of biscuits. An evening meal was specially ordered from a nearby Sri Lankan restaurant, carefully prepared with minimal oil and fat. Gradually, he felt a pleasant peculiarity and imaginary pleasantry in the company of a lady.

One day, Frazer developed backache, which was not relieved by painkillers. Molly offered to give him a back massage which went on for almost an hour. He felt better. The next evening, Molly repeated the massage. Halfway through, Frazer felt a sudden sexual surge which Molly was anticipating and sensed. Without any words being spoken, she tactfully helped him out. Then it became a nocturnal pastime and pleasure for both. Having been a lonely man after his wife's death, without any physical contact with a lady, he felt an air and aura of wondering pleasure. After three weeks, Frazer requested her to stay further. She agreed to another three weeks. By that time, he was a lot better and carrying out all the routine daily activities he undertook prior to the heart attack.

Through the restaurant contact, Molly arranged a home help. A 58-year-old Sri Lankan man who also helped part-time as a delivery driver. On the evening before leaving Australia, Frazer took Molly for a sumptuous meal in an upmarket restaurant and gave her a surprise gift, a cheque for US $5,000. Molly was overwhelmed and promised to return in three months.

8

Moving Home

With the arrival of new baby, Julie found things were gradually getting out of control. Molly was over-caring, over-reacting, overpowering and wanted to take care of the baby all by herself. Every time baby cried, Molly would come into the room, intruding the privacy of bedroom fabric. Mother and daughter were at loggerheads with each other; an age-old conflict.

Frequent arguments over trivial things became the norms of the day. In the pillow talk, Julie and Jacob agreed that three generations could not live under the same roof. So, they decided to look for another house. Molly did not like the idea. She also persuaded Mark to coax and dissuade them from moving out. But Mark prudently took a neutral stance and left it to the couple's wish and choice.

The house hunting went on for three weeks. When Jacob was discussing this with the partners at work, one of them mentioned there was a couple emigrating to New Zealand in the nearby village, who wanted a quick sale. He promised to find out details. Luckily, both Jacob and Julie liked the house. Moreover, all the fittings and furniture were in the deal.

The house was detached and impressive. It stood in a popular residential setting and enjoyed a beautiful south-facing garden. The property had been enhanced over the years and was immaculately presented. It had great character combined with many modern fittings and a particular feature was the superb master suite with its large dressing room, balcony and en-suite. The living space included two large reception rooms, breakfast room, kitchen, and utility. There was also a downstairs cloakroom. There was a pool table. The accommodation benefitted from gas central heating and double glazing.

Outside a block-set forecourt provided parking and access to the large garage. To the rear, the delightful garden combined an extensive patio lawn and an array of well-stocked borders. There was also a large greenhouse and a shed. Overall, it was a fine home in an extremely popular setting. There was trailing dark glossy ivy climbing greedily, gripping the brickwork with its twigs, and covering the whole left side of the house.

In the front garden, the thick row of conifers marked the hedge. Three nice climbers decorated the front wall. On the left, there was a honeysuckle with twining vines and dark green foliage leaves and trumpet-like flowers which were fragrant and oozed nectar that attracted hummingbirds. In the middle, there was Constance Spry rose, which was trained on trellis, with large leaves, thorns and magnificent, deeply cupped pink blossoms with myrrh fragrance. On the right, there was a jasmine with deciduous arching stems, dark green foliage, and heavily scented pentagonal white flowers.

The house move was done on a Saturday. The items were mainly clothes and personal effects since most of the furniture was left in the deal. Although Molly was not happy inside with the move, she put on a smiling face. She got them a Breville coffee maker with a grinder. Mark gave them a Samsung bar fridge with ice maker.

Jacob and Julie planned the housewarming party. For the first time in her life, Julie also planned with full freedom and without any interference from her parents. They planned to invite all staff and spouses from the law firm, close friends of

Julie and Jacob and the immediate neighbours. The practice manager organised the invitations. Altogether the head count was 38. Julie took almost full control. The basic rules were that no material gifts but cash or gift vouchers were allowed and dress to be informal. A mini bar was set up with whisky, brandy, red and white wine, gin, vodka, soft drinks, lemonade, soda water, ice etc. Titbits and hors d'oeuvres were presented. The food was a buffet arranged from a reputable firm, Lahore Tandoori Restaurant. Paper plates and disposable cutlery were set up.

Everyone started arriving from 6.30 onwards for 7 in the evening. Light music was playing. Jacob and Julie took turns to conduct a guided tour of the house in small groups. Julie was surprised and a bit embarrassed to see Charlotte among the guests. She explained that she was covering for one of the staff who was ill for two weeks. What bothered Julie more, was that she was wearing a lilac rust satin twist front open sleeve wrap dress with clover gold metallic heeled strappy sandals which were the same as Julie was wearing.

Molly happened to walk past and stopped for a moment, glanced at Charlotte with a smile and noted her large hoop golden earrings, light make-up with mascara, eye liner, lip gloss and thin blush. She complimented, 'You look beautiful.'

Julie stared at her mother-in-law in astonishment. Although Julie did not like the compliments, she just bit her lip and carried on chatting with arriving guests. She was engulfed with disquiet and restlessness inside but managed to hastily refresh and put on a smiling face. They all started drinking at leisure.

Starters were samosa, chicken pakora and king prawn butterfly. Main courses were a choice of lamb tikka, chicken makani, and prawn balti. Plenty of pilau rice, nan, salad, and pickles were at disposal. The party went well. People formed smaller caucuses enjoying drinking and eating.

By 10.30, all were called into the lounge. One of Jacob's partners, Oscar, was an amateur magician. He showed some tricks with a set of playing cards. Everybody gave him a good round of applause. Then Julie came forward and announced that there would be a bingo with £1 per ticket. To conduct, she said she would pass around numbers to all the ladies and whoever picks number 9 would have to conduct the bingo. It fell on Charlotte. She accepted the offer and did conduct the game almost like a professional.

After calling the various numbers, Julie shouted, 'I have won.'

Charlotte verified and screamed, 'Bingo' and gave her the winning jackpot of £42. Jacob asked them to pause to take some photos. Observing similar dress worn by Julie and Charlotte, one of the ladies commented,

'They look like twins.' That did not go well with Julie. Her mood of gaiety and enthusiasm suddenly turned into a nonplussed state wiping out the vibrant smile. She gazed at the lady with tinge of displeasure before walking away.

Lot of chatting and drinking continued. Men started cracking jokes. Then it was the ladies turn. They had to sing at least three songs. Charlotte and two others sang. All were well received. Finally, the party ended at the stroke of midnight.

Julie got up at 7.30 in the morning. Jacob was still asleep. She went down to have a coffee. She started feeling uneasy and irritable. By 8.30 she went back upstairs and woke Jacob. She asked him, 'Why didn't you tell me that silly bitch was coming?'

'Who?'

'You know well who it is. Charlotte.'

'I didn't know; it is the manager who invited all the staff.'

'You knew it all. I told you what I would be wearing. How come she was wearing the same?' Julie's eyes were spitting fire, her face was twitching, and teeth were grinding.

'Sorry. I had no idea what people would be wearing.'

Julie stared at him and the gaze penetrated through him like a dagger. She left angrily muttering, 'I am not putting up with this nonsense anymore.'

Jacob could not think clear. He thought, I didn't do anything wrong. Now I have to bear the cross. He looked at the mobile to see the photos he took. Charlotte appeared gorgeous and smiling while Julie was a bit sulky. He thought, when Julie sees this, she'll be even more annoyed.'

The next day, breakfast was in a mute environment. Julie went up to attend to the crying baby, halfway through breakfast.

Mark had arranged a home help through his contacts. She was called Dafina, a 68-year-old Welsh lady who lived in the nearby village. She presented as a preternaturally plausible, polite, and pleasant lady who established an instant rapport with Julie. Julie talked about the daily routine - general tidying and cleaning, kitchen care, laundry, and other jobs as needed.

Dafina got on cleaning and started with the lounge. After a couple of hours, she put the kettle on. Julie was sat in the dining room. When she made tea, Julie asked her to have a break and join her. Julie was eager to know her background.

With a deep sigh and faint smile, she said, 'When I got married, l was in Wales. The life was quite different. Very few women worked. My main job was to do all the household work and look after children. Even in secondary schools, girls were given lessons in cookery, darning, sewing and household management. We lived in a three-bedroomed house. There was no central heating; the downstairs rooms were heated by a coal fire. Upstairs the heating was from two electric heaters. We had a coal bunker. In the kitchen, we had a fridge. Nobody I knew had a freezer. There were no supermarkets. We used to get things locally from the baker, butcher, and the greengrocer. Only very few had cars. My husband was a coal miner. He had a motorbike and used to take me on the back of it on weekends.'

'Where is your husband?'

'He was a heavy smoker. He died of lung cancer when he was 56.'

'When did you come over here?'

'Eighteen years back. My second daughter got married to a train driver from Burnley. When my husband died, she wanted me to come over. She got me a job in the supermarket. I worked there 14 years.'

Dafina put the clothes in for washing. She continued with a deep sigh. 'While in Wales, we didn't have a washing machine. A neighbour had one. So I had to take it to her at her convenience. She charged for this every time. I had to get the washing out and put it out to dry or hang it on the clothes horse. I always listened to the radio while cooking. I kept asking my husband for a television. Finally, he got me a second-hand one on my birthday. The programmes were black and white. There were only two channels.'

She continued, 'Sunday night was bath night. The water was heated by a back boiler behind the coal fire or in the summer, by an expensive electric immersion heater. Hot water tanks could not store that much water, so shallow baths were the order of the day, as all the family would bathe one after the other. Most households had a vacuum cleaner and a cooker. Entertainment was provided by the radio (wireless) or gramophone, and more and more people were acquiring televisions. These, like telephones, were rented, not owned. All televisions showed programmes in black and white; there were only two TV channels to watch, the BBC and the commercial channel. Clothes were often homemade, either sewn or knitted.

Knitted items when outgrown were recycled by being unravelled and re-knitted into something else. When collars on shirts became frayed, they were unpicked, turned inside out and sewed back on. All buttons and zips from old clothes were saved for the button box. Socks and stockings were darned. Dinner would be on the table ready and waiting for the man of the house on his return from work. Housework and the care of children was considered woman's work so the man would expect the house to be clean and tidy, a meal ready, children fed and washed and his clothes all ready for the next day at work.'

Dafina carried on giving a vivid description of life in the 1950s. 'There was a succession of callers to the house. These would include the rag and bone man, a man with a horse and cart and a call of 'any old rags.' The rag and bone man would buy your old clothes for a few pennies and mend your pots and pans when the bottoms went through. There was also the 'pop man' from whom you would buy lemonade, and dandelion and burdock soda, and each week you would return your empty bottles to him when you bought your next week's drinks. Alcoholic drinks could be bought from the off-licence, often part of the local pub; again, you would return the bottles in exchange for a few pence. The milkman came daily and delivered your milk right on to your doorstep – again he would take away the empty bottles to be washed and re-used. The local shops would also deliver your groceries, bread and meat, the delivery boys used bicycles to make their rounds. The dustbin men worked extremely hard, carrying the old metal dustbins on their backs from the householder's back door to the cart and then returning them back.

'For the housewife, there was no need to go the gym. She walked to the shops and took the children to school every day on foot; the housework she did was very labour-intensive without today's gadgets and there were no such things as convenience foods or fast-food outlets. Sweets and crisps (the only flavour available was ready salted) were treats rather than everyday foods. In the 1950s, a housewife had been prepared both at school and at home for her role in life; she took pleasure and pride in looking after her home and family to the best of her ability. However, on the other side of the coin, she didn't have a career outside the home and she had no income of her own, which left her dependent on her husband.' All these stories were thought-provoking for Julie and she felt how lucky she was to be housewife in the 21st century.

Dafina enquired how she was feeling. Julie admitted that she was feeling low in mood and lost interest in things. She felt tired and lacked energy. She had trouble sleeping at night and felt drained and sleepy during daytime.

While bringing a cup of tea, Dafina casually remarked, 'I was like a sparrow stuck in the nest in my marriage. The more time my partner spent away from home and less food he brought gave me clues that he was seeing somebody else.'

Dafina thought Julie was suffering from post-natal depression, which she herself had suffered in the past. She recalled, sobbing, 'I had four children. I lost my eldest daughter in Aberfan school tragedy in 1966, where 116 children were killed. I can never get over it. Every day I think about her.'

She took a photograph from her handbag, kissed it twice and gave it to Julie. Julie looked at it sadly and stone-faced and gave it back with a deep sigh.

Julie said, 'I am losing love for my daughter.'

'Do you feel like hurting her?

'Not really; but I feel it like a burden. I can't look after her.' Julie sat leaning forward keeping her head in hands and sobbed.

Dafina tried to console her and added, 'Is it ok if I talk to

Molly about it?'

Julie kept mute and looked at her through the corners of her eyes and nodded twice in approval.

Dafina rang Molly that evening and explained the situation. While talking, Mark came on the phone and got further details. Then they both sat together and decided to visit Julie the next day about 11 in the morning. Dafina was cleaning the kitchen. Julie confided that she had pain in her left breast and could not feed the baby. Mark rang Jacob and discussed matters. He agreed that Julie should see the GP urgently.

Julie saw the GP that evening. She had a breast abscess and was put on antibiotics. She was also started on anti-depressant medication and was advised to stop breastfeeding. Mark and Molly discussed the situation. Mark felt it would be better that Julie stayed with them for four to six weeks so that the baby could be looked after well, and to allow time for Julie's breast abscess to settle down and for the antidepressant to kick in. Also, back in Sri Lanka, after childbirth, mother and baby would stay with parents for 8 to 12 weeks. It would also give Jacob a break and some relief.

The next day, Mark and Molly asked Dafina to look after the baby and took Julie and Jacob for an evening meal at King Kong Chinese Restaurant. Mark laid out the plan of action in a smooth diplomatic way. All were in agreement. Julie moved in to the parental home.

Molly was thrilled to look after the baby and be back in charge of things. Jacob also felt relief since the home situation was slipping away from him. He kept visiting Julie three times a week. Coming home, he felt lonely and bored. He started drinking more and more wine. Ten days later it was Valentine's Day. Jacob wanted to take Julie out for a meal but Julie said she didn't feel up to it. So, Jacob gave her a card and bunch of red roses. Jacob was desperate to see Charlotte. On the way back, he rang her and dropped a card and a hamper with a bottle of Prosecco, chocolate and a bunch of red roses. She wanted him to stay. Jacob briefed her about the home situation. He had a very important court case next day which needed a lot of time to prepare. So, he said he had to leave soon and promised to meet in a week's time.

A week later, Charlotte went to a Sri Lankan shop and got provisions needed to cook a meal as well as sea bass and chicken. Next day, she texted Jacob to ask if he could call in that evening. He agreed. Jacob arrived at 5.30 after work. Charlotte was wearing a khaki casual cotton linen cross backs pocket baggy apron and very little make-up.

He complimented, 'You look elegant and sexy in this outfit.'

She smiled and replied 'Thank you. You haven't fulfilled your promise.'

'What promise?'

'To teach me Sri Lankan cooking.'

He glanced at her and burst into a sudden sharp bout of laughter. He put his arm around her squeezing her shoulders and stared deeply at her from head to foot. She felt like a bubble was brewing in her bosom. She gave him a carrier bag and gave him a smirk, winked and whispered,

'Get changed. It is your turn to show me the cooking.'

Jacob got changed and came back wearing a chef's apron and headwear. Jacob said he would make Country Captain Chicken. She was very curious hearing the name and asked why it is called so.

He stayed mute with a grin and then said, 'I will show you the cooking first and then tell you the story.' He kept talking her through the various steps. The chicken was cut into small pieces. In a frying pan, two tablespoons of oil was added and put on high heat. A pinch of mustard seeds was put in and allowed to rupture by the heat. She was curious about what mustard seeds do and asked Jacob about it. He turned around and replied in a poignant and philosophical posture,

'The Kingdom of Heaven is like a grain of mustard seed, which a man took, and sowed in his field, which indeed is smaller than all seeds. But when it is grown, it is greater than the herbs, and becomes a tree, so that the birds of the air come and lodge in its branches. This is from the Gospel of Matthew.' Charlotte was stunned, speechless and stumped by his analogy.

He sliced coriander leaves, onions, red peppers, garlic and ginger and added them. After couple of minutes, garam masala powder was added. The chicken was put in, mixed well, two teaspoons of butter and a bit of salt and a glass of water were added. It could cook on a high heat for 25 minutes. The dish was done.

Charlotte reminded him about the name.

Jacob said, 'Sri Lanka was previously called Ceylon. My country was colonised by first the Portuguese, Netherlands and then by the British, who ruled for nearly 150 years. So many captains were traversing up and down the country most of the time. They would arrive and at short notice, expect a good meal. This type of curry was popular and thus called 'Country Captain.'

Then it was time to make pilau rice. He said, 'Once a cook told me that there are so many pilaus like stars in the sky. It is a quite common dish in the Middle East and Far East.' He heated olive oil in a saucepan, added long grain rice and stirred for 5 minutes. Salt, pepper, chicken stock and water were added and covered. This was left to cook at a very low heat for 30 minutes.

Charlotte bent down to get something from the fridge. Her brawny pantherine hips standing out as guards revealing the natal cleft, caused a gush of flutter in Jacob. She turned around, dropped her eyes and with a sceptical glance said,

'I am making a cocktail for my prince.' Her smile blushed into a mumble. In a shaker, she mixed apricot brandy, lemon juice, calvados, and dry gin. 'This is especially for you, my ... Prince's Smile Cocktail.'

They finished dinner and sat on the settee.

Charlotte said, 'I would like to know more about Sri Lanka.'

'It is an island separated by 30 miles of sea from India. It is incredibly beautiful.'

'A friend of mine went there last year. I saw pictures of her riding an elephant. I love elephants.' She got excited, elated, and exhilarated and suddenly jumped up in joy, raised both hands in a raise-the-roof sign.

'Have you got a passport?'

'Yes.'

She peered deep into Jacob's eyes. 'Will you take me to Sri Lanka?'

Jacob paused for a few seconds and mumbled in a soft tone, 'Yes, I will.'

He caressed her hair and shoulders, held her close to his chest and murmured in her ears, 'Promi—'

Before he could complete the word, Charlotte thrust her soft lips into his, almost swallowing the unspoken words. They embraced and stayed together for almost two hours.

9

Marriage on the Rocks

Jacob had an excessively big upset at work. He lost an important case in the court, which all the partners in the firm thought Jacob should have won. That was a longstanding client's case. There was a practice meeting after that. Two of the partners expressed their concern at Jacob's performance. Jacob felt it like a blow below the belt. It affected his morale and self-confidence.

He started working a lot more hours and would stay until eight in the night many days, to get on top of the game. When he came home, Julie would be already in bed most of the time. Dafina always kept dinner ready for Jacob. Julie's depression tablets made her drowsy. Moreover, she had lost interest in most things. She even found it difficult to keep feeding the baby since it interrupted her sleep. So Jacob fed the baby at night with her bottle. In effect, he also could not get enough sleep. The sleeplessness had a knock-on effect, Jacob started feeling tired at work and unable to concentrate.

On two occasions, when Jacob went to Julie in bed, she was not in any mood. She said the medication was making her feel like a zombie. Jacob was feeling increasingly frustrated. He did not know where to turn to. Most days, he used to sleep on the settee watching movies on TV until late. He started drinking nearly a bottle of wine every night to relax and get to sleep. As time went on, he started drinking more and more, almost two bottles of wine a night.

One of the staff at work who typed the minutes of the practice meeting, accidentally mentioned about the case Jacob lost, while chatting with another secretary. In a few weeks, there was a whispering campaign about Jacob's credibility at the staff level. Jacob started feeling increasingly frustrated. There was no peace or happiness at home. Julie was ill and not interested. The work he worshipped and loved had turned sour. He felt the staff at work were colluding against him. At work, on many days he felt moody and brooding. The practice manager smelt a rat. He alerted the senior partner, who thought it would be better to discuss with Jacob and find out what was going on.

Next week, the senior partner had a one-to-one discussion with Jacob. Jacob opened up and admitted family problems, Julie's illness and that he also was feeling low. The senior partner advised Jacob to take a week as compassionate leave and see his GP as soon as possible.

Jacob saw his GP two days later. He diagnosed Jacob as moderately depressed and referred him for counselling urgently. Since the NHS waiting list was long, Jacob chose to see a private counsellor. The GP advised him to attend a follow-up appointment after two weeks. Jacob could not stay at home. He did not want Julie to know about his problem which would only make matters worse. Moreover, if he stayed at home, he was concerned Dafina might find out about his state. Home was a cold and clammy environment and staying there during the day would be a burden and boring. Jacob went to the council library and spent an hour reading. He could not concentrate. So, he went to the pub, sat in a quiet corner, and started drinking double vodka and wine, sipping between the two. His mind was scrambled, and thoughts were fleeting.

"I have no blood relation in this country. Nobody understands my problems. I am being knocked from pillar to post. Julie does not care about me anymore. It is not just her illness. She is a changed person now. I need somebody. I could talk to Jim but being dad's friend, I would rather not do so.'

Jacob went to the bar, got another glass of wine, and ordered a jacket potato with tuna and sat down pondering the next move. He scanned through his mobile phone contacts. When he saw Charlotte's number, he felt an irresistible urge to contact her.

He texted her: How are you? Are you ok to talk?

She texted back: 'I'm at home; ok to talk.'

Jacob rang her. His voice was slurred and trembling. 'I wanted to discuss something. Is it ok with you if I pop in the next half an hour?'

'No problem. I will leave the front door key under the door mat outside; just open and come in when you arrive.'

Charlotte sensed something was seriously wrong judging from his voice. She had been ironing, cleaning, and tidying. She had not had a wash the previous day since she had felt a bit lazy. She put the water heater on, finished tidying up, put the key under the mat and went up to the bathroom. The water was only lukewarm. So, she went back, tidied the bedroom and put clothes in the washing machine and returned to the bathroom. She had a thorough, refreshing shower. After drying she wrapped herself with a light pink cotton wrap gown. She applied exceptionally light make-up and thin blush. While drying her hair, she heard the front door being opened.

She just shouted, 'I will be down in two minutes.' She did not get any response. She simply combed her long, wavy, auburn hair and left it loose lazily over her shoulders since it was not fully dry.

When Charlotte came down, Jacob was lying on the settee with his suit on, asleep snoring. His tie was slightly unfastened and there was food debris on his chin. There was a strong smell of alcohol. She felt concerned and perplexed. She thought, this can't be Jacob. Poor soul: what happened to him? She rushed and sat beside him on the settee and shook his left shoulder and called loudly,

'Jacob, Jacob; wake up.'

Jacob tried to open his eyes. His eyeballs kept rolling and closing, his head slumped back.

She asked, 'What is the matter, Jacob?'

He muttered in a slurred and low tone, 'Don't feel well; nobody loves me.'

Charlotte was bewildered. Jacob appeared sloshed. She had never seen him in this state. She pulled him firmly towards her and made him sit up, leant against her. She took off his jacket and unfastened his tie, took his shoes off, and supported him to stand up and prompted him to walk. He tried to get up, staggered and stumbled. She held him firmly onto her chest and with her right arm encircling him, gently made him walk up the steps and let him lie on her bed. She loosened his shirt buttons and belt, got a wet tissue to wipe his face, adjusted the pillows and gave him a sharp short, sweet kiss on the lips and let him rest. Soon Jacob slipped into a slumber.

She sat next to him on the bed, stooped with her head lowered in her hands and started postulating what would have happened to Jacob. Has somebody spiked his drink? How could he drive in such a plastered state? What if he had caused an accident? Has he taken something strange? A drug? An overdose? What made him say nobody loves him? Has anything gone drastically wrong in his marriage?

She felt a sharp searing pain in her chest, the muscles on her face started twitching and she burst into a torrential flood of tears which overflowed into her mouth giving a salty taste. She sank her head in her hands and cried her heart out until she got some catharsis of sorrow and sadness. Then she blotted off tears on her face and hands onto the gown, hugged Jacob and whispered in his right ear,

'I love you; I love you,' although Jacob was fast asleep.

She took two deep sighs, got up and walked gently towards the window and through the slit in the curtain kept staring at his car and stood still in sombre sentiment. She thought, the car looks fine; there is no sign of an accident. The phone was ringing downstairs. It was Jacob's mobile. She rushed to pick it up but stopped. My goodness if I answer that will wreck the marriage. She let it ring and ring. It went to voicemail. She sat on the settee with his jacket in her lap. She picked up the jacket, kissed it twice, hugged it and held it firm and rubbed it on her bare bosom over her heart.

Then a sudden thought crept in. Shall I check his pocket? I know it is private and I should not do it. But he has come to me for help. So, it is my duty to help. She checked and found the pub receipt. He'd had two vodkas, three glasses of wine - 250ml each - that is 750ml in total making it a full bottle; no wonder he was plastered. But why? She put the receipt back, sighed heavily and started sobbing, which turned her beautiful blue eyes reddish and sore.

She went up to check on Jacob. He was still fast asleep in the same position. She did not know what to do next. She paused for a few seconds, sat and hugged him, pressed her soft lips onto his forehead across his hairline and got up. Recalling her experience of nights out, she felt that the best thing was to let him sleep it off.

She could not settle; started pacing back and forth. Her mind was like a fuming volcano. Jacob had been asleep for nearly four and half hours. What made him say so when he came in. Anyway, I will make him feel loved. I will make him happy. She went down, sat on the settee while glancing at his car and made some notes on a writing pad and stayed lost in her thoughts. She put the coffee maker on and went up to get ready. Then she browsed through her wardrobe and wore a satin elegant floral baby pink spaghetti strap nightdress. She looked in the mirror. She felt her high bosoms were heating up, throbbing, and spitting fire.

Charlotte went back to wake Jacob up. She sat beside him and shook his right shoulder twice. Jacob opened his eyes and appeared to be in a daze. He sat up and looked surprised and bewildered.

He exclaimed, 'How come I am here?' He couldn't remember what happened. His eyes were bloodshot, and his mouth was sagging. He went to the bathroom, washed his face, and refreshed. There was a slight spark on his face when he came back. Charlotte pointed at the pillow and smiled. There was a wet mark 'C' on it, due to dribbled saliva from Jacob.

She quipped curiously, 'In sleep, you started writing my name C...'

He still could not fathom out how he ended up there. Charlotte did not want to have any unpleasant conversation. She thought she would leave it for another day to find out what exactly had happened.

She looked into his eyes and with a penetrating smile, winked and murmured, 'Are you happy to be with me? A solitary cherry candle in the middle of the dressing table with the words *True Love* written on was lit up, reflecting the light diffusely. 'Don't let the sun go down on me', the love song by Elton John and George Michael, was playing softly in the background. The scent from her drew him closer giving him a calm headspace. He enquired what she was wearing.

She said, 'This is Philosophy Pure Grace Fragrance. It is

refreshing with notes of lily, leafy greens, and frosted musk. It's clean, pure and fresh.'

'Just like you!'

She burst into a sudden, sharp, and slightly hysterical bout of giggles which buzzed and echoed around Jacob's ears inciting him in a whirlpool of uninhibited passion. He just could not believe his eyes and he kept on scanning her from head to foot and beyond. She was bare-footed and wearing only the nightwear. The outfit embraced her exceptionally beautiful body curves and produced a dazzling silhouette effect against the backdrop in the dimmed light. He touched her chin and gently twisted her head towards him and looked at her in remote and deep thought. The coils of her leafy, brownish-red hair tumbled and plunged all over her shoulders. The velvety eyelashes danced in tune with every movement of her slender black eyebrows and her eyes sparked, emitting deep passion. The cherry-red plump full lips were inviting and demanding.

He caressed her shoulders and arms feeling the satin like silky smooth skin, ran his fingers delicately through the coils of her hair and drew her close. Then he slowly slid his left hand down her side and got stuck in her concave and brawnilicious valley of midriff due to the projectile, pantherine hour-glass hips which were impatiently vibrant and pulsating as if getting ready for a race. She turned towards him and ran her slender velvety feather-like fingers over his beer belly. In a flash, Jacob felt proud below the navel and felt a sense of scorching heat as if the heater switch was just turned on. Soon the lips parted in eagerness to be engulfed by each other. The starter encounter lasted fifteen minutes and they slowly tumbled onto the bed to continue with the main course.

An hour and a half later, Jacob wanted to leave. He felt a grateful de-stressed feeling. He got up, went to the bathroom, and refreshed. On return, he was still smelling of alcohol. Charlotte thought he was still much over the limit and should not be driving. He was in two minds. She insisted he took a taxi home and Jacob obliged.

It was 10.30 at night when Jacob got home. Julie was in bed but still awake.

As soon as he walked in Julie questioned, 'Where were you? I rang you twice.'

He turned towards her and replied in a soft apologetic and despondent tone, 'I had a bad day. The car broke down. It needed some spare part to fix. I had to get a taxi.'

'So, where is the car now?'

His legs trembled and voice fluttered, 'At the RT Garage.'

As he walked past the smell cocktail of alcohol and unfamiliar perfume reached Julie's nostrils like unwanted progeny. She felt he was being evasive. But she couldn't be bothered to challenge him or pick up a fight.

Jacob got changed and went down to the lounge, laid on the settee and while watching TV, he slept. In the morning by 8.30 Jacob got a taxi. He went to McDonald's and had a lazy breakfast, reading his newspaper. Then he went and picked the car up.

Julie wanted to check. Sharply after nine, she rang the RT Garage. Both Jacob and Julie used to take their cars there for servicing. So she knew the staff well. She made a polite enquiry.

'This is just to check when Jacob's car will be ready?'

The workman James was not sure. He asked her to hold on, checked and told her that the car was not here. She gave the registration number to countercheck and again he confirmed. Julie went into a rage. She was fuming and started pacing up and down. Dafina just knocked on the door and walked in. Seeing Julie's state, she made a polite enquiry about what was bothering her. Julie narrated all the matters. She was still in a mad state.

Dafina made tea and wanted to calm Julie down. She went up to Julie who was sat on the dining chair, patted her on the shoulders and said, 'When I was 27, I came to know my husband had an affair with my neighbour's wife. In fact, it was she who started it all, when he went to repair their coal bunker. Her husband was an alcoholic and he was not bothered at all. He spent all his money and time in the pub.'

'Then, what happened?'

'I had to put up with all that. One day there was a bust up between them while drinking in the pub. The police were called when he threatened to slash my husband's neck with a broken bottle. They both were given a stern telling-off by the police. That was the end of it.'

Julie didn't know how to deal with the situation. She rang a close friend Christine who had had some marital problems in the past. Christine advised her to keep a diary of what was going on for a week and then discuss how to proceed. She reminded her not to confront Jacob straightaway since he may feel threatened and act in a defensive manner.

Julie started observing Jacob more carefully. He seemed distant when he came home. Christine advised her to employ a private detective to monitor Jacob's movements, which she did. But after three weeks, Julie could not get any useful information. She decided to stop and see how things were going.

The workload was dragging Jacob steadily down. He felt there was too much on his plate. Secretary Maxine had a car crash. She sustained a fractured pelvis and left forearm. She underwent an operation and was likely to be off work for possibly four months. It was not easy to get good bank staff with legal training. Jacob found it difficult to do all the administration work since his share was handled by different secretaries on different days in Maxine's absence. This was already compounding to his woes at work. One of the secretaries mentioned that she knew a lady called Wendy, who lived in the next street and used to work with a firm of solicitors. She did not know more about her but agreed to find out.

Two days later she got details of Wendy. The manager called her in for a chat. Wendy was 38, divorced over two years ago and had work experience as a legal secretary for eight years. She appeared well-versed with legal affairs, use of legal jargon, usage and typing of legal texts. She was working on a temporary basis as a part-time library assistant two and half days a week. The manager offered her work five days per week, for a period of three months on a temporary basis, with the possibility of extension. Wendy seized the opportunity with both hands.

Wendy was incredibly attractive, lissom, brisk in movements and gifted with impeccable manners. She started on a Monday. The manager briefed her regarding the work and about Jacob. She was shown around the office and was introduced to other staff. By 11 in the morning, she was taken to her desk and was logged onto her computer. She noticed a big pile of files on the desk, which the other secretaries had gleefully left for her to deal with since they were Jacob's cases. Jacob had court duty in Peterborough that day. Wendy dealt with most of the backlog work and put coloured stickers in some files - queries to clarify with Jacob. During her lunch break, she sat in the common room and got chatting with the other secretaries. She was curious to know more about Jacob's personality, his likes, and dislikes.

The next day, Wendy came to work at 8.30, half an hour early. She made sure Jacob's desk was neat and tidy. Jacob duly arrived at the office at quarter to nine. While switching on the computer, the multi-coloured stickers jutting out of the files caught his attention. Soon he got the aroma of coffee penetrating his olfactory system. After a gentle knock on his door, Wendy breezed into the room in a smooth choreographed motion, with a warm and winning smile, armed with a cup of coffee in her right hand.

She said, 'Good morning, Sir.'

Jacob stood smiling and shook her hand. 'Welcome to my office.' The light scent she was wearing emitted a delicate floral smell of white blossoms in the breeze when she walked in triggering an encounter between vanity and beauty.

Jacob had a sip of the coffee. His smile transformed into laughter. 'This is the best coffee I have tasted in my life.' He thought, she is stunning. She looks only 28; maybe 29, not even 30.

Wendy looked exquisitely groomed, wearing a light blue Jersey blouse and maroon pleated skirt which moved rhythmically. Her blue eyes sparked brilliantly through carefully manicured eyebrows and her smooth-flowing auburn hair. Jacob felt spellbound, speechless and caught up in a trance.

Sensing that, Wendy enquired, 'Sir, you like the coffee. I brought it from home especially for you. The girls in the office told me that you are a coffee lover and have six cups a day.'

'Maybe I drink a bit too much of coffee. What type of coffee was this one?'

Wendy said, 'It is Barista, well balanced, with a rich mouth feel, great body, fine taste and nice aroma.'

Looking at her through the corner of his eyes Jacob said in a gentle voice with a tender look and gestured her to sit down, 'I am not sure about these terms; can you tell me more?'

She leant forward, rested her elbows on the table and with a flickering faint smile she explained, 'The four features of coffee rating are flavour, aroma, body and acidity.'

He glanced at her. 'Sounds interesting. It is too technical for me to understand.'

'Body is the term for how thick and flavoursome a coffee is. Columbian coffee is well known for its body. In other words, if it does not linger on your palate, it does not have body. Slightly citrus acidity is desirable in well-balanced coffee.' Wendy gave a succinct and quick rundown.

'What do you mean by well-balanced?' He enquired inquisitively and leant towards her corner, rubbing his hands.

'It means that no one particular flavour dimension is dominant, acidity or body like most central American and African coffee. Also, the Latin American coffee is famous for being free from flavour defects; we call it 'clean' in coffee terms. Naturally processed coffee has much fruitiness.' She got up. When she finished, Jacob glanced at her in full approval, He continued to appreciate discreetly, without embarrassing her. She felt the heat of Jacob's prying eyes.

Jacob asked her to sit down. He got relevant details of her past work experience. Jacob laid out the *modus operandi* of his work schedule. It looked like there were no major surprises.

'I had problems with different staff dealing with my work on different days. I am pleased that we have found somebody who can pay full attention to my work. You should be able deal with my workload without any problem.' Jacob smiled.

Wendy left saying, 'Hope so. See you, Sir.'

Jacob had a feeling of sudden offloading some burden he had been carrying since Maxine went off sick. He also felt something strange - a pleasurable sensation of intrusion and infringement into his inner territory, like a friendly cat trespassing into his dwelling.

Two weeks later, Wendy had a flat tyre in the morning. She rang the AA and waited for an hour but they said there would be another thirty minutes' delay. So she got a taxi since she didn't want to be late for work. That evening, Jacob dropped her off at home. She invited him for coffee but he said,

'Not now; I 've got something to sort out this evening, sorry.' He waved and drove off slowly since some kids were kicking a football on the street. He could see her in the rear mirror, stood up, half-waving and half-gazing at Jacob's car. While in the car, a rainbow of emotions started filling his mind.

On returning home, he went to bed soon after dinner. At about 10.45, Julie came in and gently stroked and caressed him to wake him up.

Jacob said, 'Sorry, darling; I have a bad headache.' Then he turned away and lay feigning sleep. Julie did not think much about it much since she also had her off days.

Wendy was off one week. The Wednesday was Jacob's birthday. The staff organized a small get-together with a cake, titbits, and sandwiches at lunchtime in the office. The next week, Wendy surprised Jacob with an invitation saying,

'I am going to cook a meal for you tomorrow evening as a special birthday treat.'

Jacob said, 'Tomorrow I am not free.'

'Which other day can you make?'

'Day after tomorrow is fine.'

'Ok, thanks.'

'I will come for a drink; no need to prepare a meal.'

'That is fine; see you then.'

Jacob arrived at half past six in the evening, bang on time. On pressing the doorbell, Wendy strolled to open the door with a soft, loving look, her shoulders back, chin up and she made instant, spontaneous eye contact. She stood holding the half-open door and greeted politely,

'Welcome home.'

Wow; what a sight; she is dressed to kill, Jacob thought in sheer astonishment.

Wendy was wearing a strawberry-red drape neck open back side-slit party dress and matching patent leather stiletto heel pumps. She turned around, wiggled her hips and took a few small steps. Her small waist, rounded hips and butt danced in rhythm in front of Jacob. He felt blinded by her beauty and stunning appearance. He dreamed of her hot body.

The red synthetic ruby pendant necklace and elegant pear cut briolette drop cubic Zirconia diamond earrings sparkled and dazzled in the light as she moved. Her downy blonde hair highlighted with strawberry red strands and the luxurious curls were draped over her arms. The scarlet red dimpled cheeks smiled on their own.

Eyes are the windows to the soul, Jacob felt, as the eye language gave out more vibes than her whole body. Her blue eyes sparkled like emeralds. The upper and lower lash lines defined her eyes. There was a sweep of burnt rose-gold eyeshadow over the lids extending the shade toward the outer corners and under the bottom lashes. Her vibrant poppy shade lips with blurred edges along the lip line appeared fresher and emanated much sex appeal. The rest of her face appeared clean and dewy.

Jacob was bedazzled by her vibrant smile, sparkling eyes and the flowing hair. Wendy scored ten out of ten for the seductive date-night make-up that glowed in the light. She carried herself well and looked comfortable in her skin – she exuded sex appeal.

The silver Pandora birthday cake was smiling at Jacob. He blew off the candles and cut the cake while Wendy was clapping and singing 'Happy Birthday'.

Wendy gave him a kiss on his cheek and gave the card which read:

Happy Birthday
Jaunty ***A***vant-garde ***C***aring ***O***pulent ***B***reezy!
Wendy xx

Then she gave him a gift bag which had a blue and pink luxury floral silk tie and with matching cufflinks. Jacob was gobsmacked.

Through the back window, the landscape of woody hills caught Jacob's attention.

Wendy quipped, 'That is a beautiful scene.'

Jacob turned towards Wendy, peered into her eyes and with a grin, whispered, 'I have found something much more beautiful.'

'What?'

'I can see it with my eyes; it is just right in front of me but you can't see it with your eyes.' Jacob grinned.

'What do you mean?'

'You; yourself.'

Wendy blushed momentarily with a pleasant pallor of being praised right on the face. The words resonated indelibly in her ears.

She brought a bottle of Henriot Reims Champagne, nicely chilled and two elegance coupe champagne glasses. He developed a sudden urge to share the drink with her. He thought, After all, my birthday comes only once a year.

They both stood up, smiled, stared into each other's eyes, raised the full coupes and clinked the glasses.

Wendy said, 'I toast the birthday of the best gentleman I have ever met. May you continue to grow in your wisdom.'

Jacob gazed at her with admiration. He was thoroughly impressed with her warm manners and demeanour. Jacob pondered and threw a quick glance at her bosom which was threatening to gain freedom by breaking open through the open- neck dress. They both sat down on the settee with their drink.

Wendy felt an accent of deep passion to be cuddled and fondled by a gentleman for whom she had feelings, which she had been longing, craving, and dreaming about for a while. The moment was so near within her grasp and in the catchment territory of her breath. Her heart started fluttering, palms sweating, and lips trembling. The messages went back and forth across the hearts and minds. Jacob felt the reverberations transmitting onto himself making goose pimples. He accidentally spilled a bit of champagne on his shirt. Wendy briskly got some tissue and blotted it off in the most delicate and soft gesture, rubbing over his heart attempting to rob it in whole or part of it. Jacob held her hand for a moment, looked at Wendy through the corners of his eyes, making a rendezvous with her blue eyes, and his inner self went into a meltdown. A feeling of sudden paralysis of his functions and an urge for bodily closeness took over him. The lytic cocktail of Wendy's Elizabeth Arden perfume ignited in the warmth of her breath leaving calling cards on his neck, and drove him into an unchartered and unexplored territory of dreamland. The rhythmic movements of her high bosoms signalled the desire to explode onto him, seeking, pleading, and begging to be explored.

Jacob's throat went dry. He wanted to talk but the words were stuck and not wanting to be spoken. He did not know how to express his emotion or care either how things would transform. He felt hapless and helpless, like being electrocuted by the high voltage charge generated by Wendy and trapped in the mesmerizing grasp of a lady wanting every bit of him, in exchange for offering her at his feet. Jacob wanted to say something to break the silence, but his voice quivered in the frolicking gaze of Wendy. The transient confusion of who should make the first move, hung over them in suspended animation.

Wendy put the drink on the coffee table, leaned forward with an intense desire to engulf Jacob, gently put her arms around his shoulders and pulled him forward, pressing her throbbing bosom onto him and pinching the nape of his neck. The hairs on his neck stood up. His half-smiling demeanour with partly open mouth and adoring glimpse was the gate pass to thrust her fleshy lusty lips into his. Jacob's sensory system went into overdrive while Wendy's motor system followed suit. Wendy hugged him hard and gently thrust her body onto him succumbing him to lay on the settee. They lay intertwined like snakes. Jacob visualized the Titanic of his marital vows sinking after being hit by the iceberg – the rock hard, determined and enterprising Wendy.

The lingering loveliness of moments caught in the avalanche of turbulent emotions, mirrored the Romeo and Juliet scene. The tempo was rudely interrupted by the chiming of the clock nine times dictated in unmistakable terms.

'I need to be home by 10,' Jacob muttered.

He glanced at a picture hanging on the wall of two grouses about to dance with their black wings spread out, white tail aquiver and red wattles engorged.

She quipped, 'Let us dance together.'

Jacob had very little experience in dancing. Also, he was a bit shy to expose his lack of dancing skills. Wendy smelt it. So, she said,

'I will dance first and you be the audience; at the end I will get you to dance together.' Then she put tango music on, went to hold Jacob by the hand and started dancing. She swayed with Jacob as the beat picked up pace, the elbows swung through the air in perfect rhyme with her feet. With one arm outstretched, her waist jerked vivaciously and with the other arm held on to Jacob gracefully and stylishly. By quarter to ten, Jacob said he wanted to leave. Wendy obliged although her heart wanted him to stay all night. She knew that was not possible now, although she longed that will turn into reality in the future. Jacob reluctantly said goodbye and left gently. Wendy stood still with her right hand waving gracefully to say 'bye', until the car disappeared from her eye line. Wendy lay dreaming on the settee and lost count of time. At the stroke of two, she set the alarm for 6.30 and went to bed.

When Jacob got home, Julie was waiting with his dinner all ready on the table.

As soon as Jacob got home, he said, 'It was a hectic day; I had some problems at work.' He sat down with Julie and ate the dinner quickly. He was comparatively less vocal at dinner. He gave a kiss to Julie while in the kitchen saying, 'I am shattered; going to bed now,' and went up. Julie felt something strange. Jacob was smelling of alcohol. She knew Jacob did not drink much. Also, she got a penetrating smell of lady's perfume which was different to hers. She thought she would let him rest tonight and talk to him next day.

Jacob left for work as usual at about 7.45 in the morning. Julie was tidying up the room and took the dirty linen for washing. She always used to check the pockets for anything before putting it in the washing machine. While checking Jacob's shirt which he was wearing the previous day, she noted a lipstick mark on the collar. She felt spooky. This is the third strange thing to happen. She grew suspicious. Instead of putting that shirt aside for the wash, she put it in a carrier bag and kept it aside.

Jacob reached the office at quarter to nine as usual. Wendy

was waiting with the coffee. This time the coffee was served with a sharp short kiss and a quick compliment.

'I thoroughly enjoyed last night. How about you?'

'I did indeed.'

'Bye for now.' While Wendy was walking to her room, she turned back, winked and landed a flying kiss on Jacob.

Jacob felt very restless inside, a sense of sensual pleasure at its zenith. He started re-living his exhilarating experience with Wendy like a cow chewing its cud. Cows regurgitate food back into their mouths so that they can 're-masticate' it. The reasoning behind this is that the extra chewing helps the cow break down fibrous forages and roughage more efficiently. He did it to enjoy the leftovers of that night of unforgettable excitement to the last nanosecond.

Jacob started dreaming of his desire and longing for a personal relationship with Wendy. Nobody, not even Julie, had managed to intrude into his heart with such lightning speed and deep conviction.

What is happening, he thought? Am I being swept away by the turbulent tidalwave of passion reigning over reason? Do I need to pull myself back on track? He thought it over and left a bit early for lunch. He went to the council library and sought out books on love and psychology. Although he wanted to read at ease, he could not read it at home. So, he decided to keep it in his drawer at the office. He could not concentrate.

He was caught in a trance. I was thrown up on top of the moon by a stunning beauty and she won't let me get back to earth. Although she has stepped into the inner rhythm of my family, I cannot blame her. I do like her. She is unique. She has an incredibly special place in my heart. I feel jealous of her hairbrush; I feel jealous of the sweat on her skin.'

When Jacob returned home that evening, Julie felt he was a

bit aloof. She wanted to know more about what had happened the previous night. Jacob narrated that there was a practice meeting of all the partners and staff in the law firm, followed by titbits, snacks and drinks. Julie threw it in his face that there was lipstick mark on his collar. Although he felt frozen for a few seconds, regaining composure, he put in an apologetic tone,

'I must admit that I tasted champagne last night, and it got to my head. Maybe when the staff were leaving, they all hugged and said "bye". I can't recollect; there were lots of people.' Julie took it at face value. Though she was not convinced, she did not want to push the issue further.

In the office, one of the secretaries, Susan, had made a serious mistake in drafting a case for the court. The mistake was spotted by Jacob who was acting for his colleague while on holiday. Because of the nature of the matter, he reported it to the manager of the firm to deal with the issue. The manager investigated and put her on a warning. Susan felt an instant dislike for Jacob. She aired it out to colleagues in the common room during tea break. Knowing the gravity of the issue, Wendy fiercely defended Jacob. The aftermath was a slowly mounting gossip campaign linking Wendy and Jacob. The manager and other partners in the firm came to know about it. Since there were no work-related issues, they brushed it aside. But the bandwagon continued to gain momentum after Susan got the sniff that Wendy spends too much time in the office, well over her scheduled hours because of Jacob. Gossips are parasitic, like leaches thriving by sucking other's blood.

Jacob and Wendy discussed the situation. They decided to meet strictly outside the office out of sight of the prying eyes of the colleagues. They kept on meeting fortnightly and used to spend about three to four hours together. It was three months since Wendy started working at Jacob's office. Maxine made a good recovery. She could come back on reduced hours with a pair of crutches, which meant Wendy's hours were cut down to twelve per week. After four weeks, Maxine resumed full-time duties resulting in the termination of Wendy's job. It was a disappointment for both Jacob and Wendy.

While Jacob had turbulence in his office, there was continued trouble at home as well. One evening, when Jacob returned from work about seven in the evening, Julie did not come down at all. The cleaner who normally leaves by five, stayed on. As soon as Jacob arrived, she told him that Julie was not well and was in bed. Jacob went straightaway. Julie said she had tummy pain and had felt sick since the afternoon. She had taken some painkillers and was resting. Jacob let her rest and went down to have dinner. Then he watched the news on TV and went up. Julie was asleep. Jacob didn't want to disturb. He took pillows and a quilt and went downstairs to lie on the settee and watch TV. He gradually fell asleep.

By about two in the morning, Julie called him. He ran up. Julie was in distress. The tummy pain got worse, and she had developed some bleeding. Jacob called the GP who came down to visit within an hour. The doctor examined her and said it looked like inflamed gall bladder and admitted her straightaway to hospital. By six in the morning, Julie underwent an operation; the gallbladder was removed. Both were deeply upset. Jacob took leave from work for the rest of the week. Julie was kept in hospital since she was feverish. The wound got infected and needed further treatment. She was discharged home after six days.

Jacob kept informing Wendy about the developments. Wendy was terribly upset and concerned about Julie's plight. But she did not want to poke her nose in, just in case matters turned worse for Jacob. On return from hospital, Julie felt extremely low and lethargic. Jacob thought it was understandable after the trauma she had been through. Julie became disinterested in things; she spent most of the time in bed. When Jacob returned from work, Julie didn't want to know.

Two weeks later, Jacob took Julie to her GP. The doctor arranged some blood tests and told Julie she was severely depressed and started her on antidepressant medication and referred for counselling. Jacob also felt rough and troubled, irritable, and moody. Mark and Molly went to see Julie. They felt that Julie could not manage the situation and look after the baby as well. They suggested that Julie stay with them for a while to recuperate. They stayed on until Jacob returned from work. Jacob also agreed with the arrangement.

Wendy used to enquire about the events at home. Two days later, she asked Jacob to drop in at her home after work. Wendy was incredibly supportive. While chatting Jacob started sobbing; he broke down in tears. He felt frozen and sat motionless gazing vacantly. Wendy helped him to stand up and held him tight to her and guided him to go upstairs. He was trembling and dizzy; he held on to the banister and reached the bedroom. As soon as he saw the bed he almost collapsed instantly like a deflated balloon. Wendy took his tie off, unfastened his shirt buttons, took his shoes off and adjusted the pillows carefully so that Jacob was comfortable. She wiped his tears with a tissue, gave him a kiss and told Jacob to chill out for a few minutes.

Wendy went to bathroom, had a quick shower, and put on make-up. She returned and gently stroked Jacob. When Jacob opened his eyes, he was mesmerized by the sight. Wendy was wearing a sexy, long, rose, transparent sheer mesh nightdress, sat beside, and leaning over him. The pair of curved, smooth and ravenous breasts dancing rhythmically with every breath of Wendy, threatened to engulf him. Her warm smile penetrated deep into his inner quarters. Jacob momentarily lost complete control and all inhibitions. He pulled her gently onto him with both hands. They had a wonderful couple of hours together. Jacob felt a lot better in himself, put on his usual patent smile and left.

Wendy took up some part-time work at the local library. Her mind was set on Jacob. They kept in touch almost daily. She had a burning desire to have Jacob's baby without anyone in the world knowing about it. She went to her GP saying that she was in a new relationship and wanted to check her fertility status since she was 38.

The doctor complimented that, 'You look like a 28-year-old rather than 38.' He arranged blood tests and later told her that she had no fertility problems.

One day, she invited Jacob for a meal. Although Jacob pretended to be reluctant, Wendy was insistent that she wanted to be with him. They went out for a Chinese meal and returned. Wendy had bought a bottle of champagne and kept in the fridge.

She stated jokingly that, 'We must get drunk tonight and enjoy it to the best, free from all bonds.'

Jacob had a slightly upset tummy. So he just had only couple of drinks. Wendy had been drinking since the afternoon. She appeared plastered. While chatting, she embraced Jacob with her podgy hands and murmured with a singular fixed look,

'I would like to have your baby.' That sent a shudder through Jacob's spine. Jacob felt trapped and petrified. He felt that it was time to end the relationship. But he did not know how to handle the situation. If he told her straightaway, he was scared that would upset her too much. Although he wanted to talk his way out, the words died away on his tongue.

He kept brooding over the issue for a few days. Then he got a call from Lilly telling him that Pinto had been admitted to hospital with a suspected stroke. He wanted to go to Colombo and see his dad. He rang Wendy about Pinto and explained that he was going away to see him. Thus, there came a natural break to end the relationship. Pinto went to Colombo for three weeks.

Jacob visited Pinto in hospital. He gradually improved and was discharged home after a week. He was put on medication. Jacob arranged for a private physiotherapist to come home and attend to Pinto. After stabilizing the situation, Jacob flew back to England.

10

Domestic Strife

A month later, Mark and Molly went away for a week, on a church pilgrimage trip to Rome. When they came back, to their horror, they found that the house had been burgled. The safe had been opened. The news spread a deep sense of shock and gloom in the house. Molly had kept gold jewellery worth 45 sovereigns, an Omega watch and ten thousand pounds in the safe. Also, there were the title deeds of properties. They prayed to St Antony for the safe return of all lost goods.

She contacted the police. There were no leads, and the police enquiry did not bear any fruits. Jacob was helping Molly with the ongoing matters. A letter arrived with a covering note: *While walking my dog in the park, I found these title deeds lying around. I am sending it to you finding your address from another torn envelope.' Mrs Romney.*

Possibly the burglars were dividing the spoils of their loot and while counting the cash, they did not bother with the documents. On checking the deed, Jacob's name was nowhere to be found. This compounded the problems into a new territory. Before his marriage, Jacob was told by Mark that the property was in the name of Molly and Julie and on marriage, Jacob's name would be added. Jacob trusted the in-laws and never thought anything further in that regard. Jacob was terribly upset, and he spoke to Mark. Mark shrugged his shoulders and said he did not know anything about it and Molly should have sorted it out. Jacob rang Molly in Colombo. She said soon after marriage, she had entrusted her niece to sort it out with the land registry. But, from the very casual and laid-back way she responded, Jacob knew things were hanky-panky. He thought he would wait until the current pandemonium was over.

Molly made various enquiries, but the mission was futile. She changed all the locks and got a security firm to put in CCTV and an alarm. A few days later, Jacob dropped in, made her a cup of tea and went into kitchen to raise the matter. She said,

'This is not the right time to discuss,' and brushed him off.

Two weeks later, it was Molly's 70th birthday. Jacob and Julie planned everything and took the whole family to King Kong Chinese Restaurant for the birthday party. The party went fine. They returned by 11.30pm. The next day, Molly woke up about 8.30 complaining of stomach pain and vomiting. She had a high temperature also. Jacob requested the GP make a home visit. The GP came about 1.30 in the afternoon. By that time, Molly was feeling worse. The GP said she had food poisoning and issued treatment. Molly stayed in bed for two days.

The second day, when the cleaner, Edith, went into her room, Julie overheard the conversation. Molly told Edith that the doctor said she had food poisoning; maybe Jacob might have put something in her drink or food since nobody else was ill. Julie was very upset to hear that. That evening, Jacob was late coming home; he had a meeting. Jacob went straight into Molly's room to see how she was. Hearing his footsteps, Molly turned away, covered her face with blanket and pretended to be asleep. Jacob had some problem at work and didn't look happy. Julie thought it was better not to tell him about Molly's conversation with Edith which could trigger a feud with his mother-in-law.

Ten days later, Jacob was returning from work. It was about

6.30 in the evening. There was patchy fog. Brooding over the domestic quagmire, while taking a turning, suddenly he saw a car in the middle of the road. Bang! The cars collided. Luckily, no injuries. Both Jacob and the other driver, a lady aged 25, were quite upset. After exchanging addresses and insurance details, he rang the AA who came, checked the car, and said it was not in a drivable state and they towed the car to PK Garage, Jacob's usual one. Later the mechanic said the car was a write-off and asked Jacob to liaise with the insurance company. So, there was a cavalcade of chaos with churlish consequences.

Jacob and Julie started looking around to buy a new car. They found a nice silver Chevrolet. That evening, while having dinner, Jacob told Mark and Molly about the new car he was planning to buy. Molly jumped in and ruled,

'If you buy that car, I will never get into that; it is below our standard. The shopkeepers have those sorts of cars. I would like my son-in-law to be driving a Volvo.' The ruling was passed. Jacob had no say or no choice.

A week later, he went into the Volvo garage, took some photos of the cars and came home. Molly liked the silver Volvo 340 car. Jacob bought it on hire purchase on Saturday morning. Soon after lunch, Molly wanted to go on a drive to church. Julie was joining them. Molly almost sprinted straight like a guided missile elbowing Julie to overtake her and jumped into the front seat. On the way, she was navigating Jacob to take a different route to the church. En route, Molly made sure she was smiling throughout and waving with monotonous regularity to imaginary friends in the nearby dwellings. When they reached the church, Fr Thomas was talking to a parishioner in the car park. As soon as the car stopped, Molly tried to eject herself from the car but she forgot the seat belt was fastened. She got out and gave a running commentary about the car and asked Fr

Thomas to bless the car. He obliged duly. She left a crisp £20 note for the favour.

***

Molly made a plea to Jacob to take her to Leicester to buy a new saree to attend the wedding of the daughter of her friend. Jacob had a lot of assignments at work so he could not go. Molly was not happy that Jacob could not come. Julie took her to Leicester. Molly bought an expensive long seamless, heavy silken green saree with golden borders.

11

Illness Strikes

Mark developed an irritating cough for two weeks. He did not take much notice and treated it as a common cough and cold. He went to the chemist to get some cough linctus. The chemist enquired about smoking. Mark smoked one Louixs cigar at Christmas and one on his birthday. He did it more as a show-off. The cigar is awfully expensive and made in Nicaragua. With Rosado wrappers, the cigar is quite hefty with a 60-ring gauge and 6-inch length. The royal stogies have notes of cocoa and spice and sport a band featuring a lovely portrait of Louis XIV, the French King. The chemist was not bothered and considered him a rare smoker. He gave some cough linctus. However, he suggested that if it did not settle down in two weeks, Mark should see his GP. On both occasions when he smoked, he would drink a 'Los Angeles Cocktail' which was composed of Canadian Club Whisky, Italian Vermouth, lemon juice, egg and sugar. He would normally narrate his pleasant experiences of his visit to Los Angeles vividly.

The cough did not settle down. During the night, Mark was up many times with the cough disturbing his sleep. Also, he felt generally weak, and his appetite was low. Molly noted he was losing weight. She persuaded him to see the GP. He was diagnosed with having a chest infection and prescribed a one-week course of antibiotics. His cough did not ease at all. After two weeks, he saw the GP again, who arranged a chest X-ray.

Two days later, the GP rang him and asked to see him urgently. The X-ray revealed a shadow in the lung suggestive of lung cancer. Mark was referred urgently to the specialist. The specialist arranged further investigations including scans.

Mark was told that he had small cell lung cancer and it had already spread. After a lengthy discussion, the specialist advised chemotherapy. By chemotherapy, drugs circulate in the bloodstream around the body. So, they can treat cells that have broken away from the lung tumour and spread to other parts of the body. Chemotherapy is the main treatment for small cell lung cancer. Doctors use it because this type of cancer responds very well to chemotherapy. Small cell lung cancer tends to have spread beyond the lung when it is diagnosed in most cases.

Mark felt very tired most of the time. His appetite was extremely poor and felt repeatedly nauseous. He started losing weight and hair. The cancer support team took over the care. Carers started coming twice daily. Over two months Mark's condition steadily deteriorated. Looking after Mark took its toll on Molly.

She started drinking heavily to cope - mainly gin and tonic, because it did not smell, and people around wouldn't get suspicious. She would fall asleep in the afternoons, which she said was due to poor diabetic control and the change in her medications. Her close friend in the church, Kathy, noted that something was certainly going wrong with Molly. She talked to her at length and found out about the alcohol problem.

Kathy went with her to see the GP. After a long discussion, Molly agreed to contact Alcoholics Anonymous as the first step, which was confidential also. It is an international mutual aid fellowship with the stated purpose of enabling its members to 'stay sober and help other alcoholics achieve sobriety.' AA is non-professional, self-supporting, and apolitical. Its only membership requirement is a desire to stop drinking.

Molly started attending AA meetings weekly. Things were getting a bit easier. On the third week, she met a 28-year-old painter in the same group. He was Cliff, five feet eight inches tall, hench and defined, with light ginger hair in a fade and taper style with chin-curtain facial hair extending from sideburns down the chin line and no moustache. He struck accord with Molly when they met first. Two weeks later, Molly invited him for a coffee after the meeting in the neighbouring café. Cliff said he did not have any money on him.

Molly replied, 'No problem; it is my treat.'

Coffee outings were great, because they allowed people to meet in a casual, no frills setting and focus on what's important, getting to know each other. If either party isn't feeling the vibe, it's easy to bow out. Molly liked the most important factor in selection - the coffee shop's spatial dynamic. Since her goal was to get to know her date, she picked a place where she could talk freely.

Molly steered clear of talking about family and relationships. She tried not to dig too deep. She was just trying to get a feeling of who Cliff was and to share in kind. The conversations were often more about feeling than information exchange. When the bill arrived, Molly pulled her purse out and flashed a fifty pound note at the waitress. She said that the manager was not in, and only he could accept that note. So, Molly put a twenty pound note in and left two pounds as a tip for a bill of £5.60. Cliff was a silent observer of this encounter.

As agreed, they met again at the same venue two weeks later. They both opened up. Cliff was single, had a girlfriend who left him 18 months back, non-smoker and drinks an occasional lager. He was a painter-come-handyman with little earnings and lived in a rented flat. Molly narrated her assets in England and Sri

Lanka and displayed her opulent lifestyle by showing him various photos on her mobile. Molly had not been in a physical relationship for three years since Mark became seriously ill. She was craving for a man as a stop-gap without any attachments. Here was the right candidate. Molly thought she should display the card now to get a feel of what she is after.

The coffee dates would last about an hour or two. At that point, there was enough time to figure out what was next. There was a lot of hubbub about who should pay, but ultimately Molly simply grabbed the initiative. One day, Molly surprised him with a gift, a Ted Baker leaf print cotton shirt in light blue. Cliff felt apologetic that he did not have anything to offer.

Molly replied in a subdued tone, 'I don't care about money or gifts; please don't bother. I very much like your company. You are really the right sort of man I was waiting for.' Cliff could not take all these on. He gazed towards the passing train and sighed, stayed silent.

Reading his indecision, Molly held his hand, leaned towards him and with a gleaning smile asked, 'Do you like Sri Lankan food?'

'Yes, I love it.'

'I have some visitors from Sri Lanka at home. Shall I pop in next Tuesday evening to your flat? I will bring some nice food; also, do not bother to get any drink. I will bring some along.'

The deal was done.

Cliff went to his flat, did a thorough clean. No lady had stepped in his flat for 18 months or so. Since he didn't know much about flowers, he asked the florist's opinion. The florist told him that red meant romance, yellow reflected the warmth and fun of enjoying another person's company, laughing at the same jokes and sharing similar interests. Cliff picked yellow roses.

On Tuesday, Molly arrived on time. Cliff opened the door and as soon as Molly sat down, offered her the bouquet of roses. Molly knew exactly the significance since she had good knowledge about flowers. She thought, this is the right one; I didn't want red roses; I just want a causal relationship with no strings attached. I need the man in him.

Cliff did watercolour paintings and sold them at Saturday markets for between £35 and £50. He showed her the paintings he had done - an active volcano with crimson red bubbling magma spitting fire, a splendorous waterfall and lakeside scene with a docked boat.

He started, 'I used to go for walks in the mountains spending a lot of time in solitude searching for inner peace and divine enlightenment. My mother was Catholic. I thought of joining a religious order to renounce the world. I am a very reserved and shy person. I feel nervous in the company of any lady.' His dwelling looked like a hovel almost akin to a hostel.

She had brought pink gin for her and Prosecco for him. They started drinking sat on the settee. Halfway through, Molly said she'd had a bit of back ache the last couple of days and turned away pointing to where the pain was. Cliff spontaneously started rubbing her back. Molly said she would lie down. She was escorted into the bedroom. Cliff started with a gentle rub on her back, which progressively escalated in intensity. More undressing was done shortly, and they ended up in bed together having a wonderful time. Molly left very satisfied. Cliff also felt that he was able to live up to her expectations. The relationship continued on an irregularly regular basis.

One day, Molly got a text from Cliff to see her urgently. She agreed to drop at his flat that afternoon at three. As soon as she sat down, he said the landlord had been on the phone twice, three months' rent was in arrears. He had been threatened with eviction unless the arrears were cleared soon. He promised to pay back the money in two months. Molly was taken aback. Regaining her composure, she enquired the amount due. It was £1,050. She pondered for a couple of minutes. Then she asked for details of the bank account of the landlord. Cliff was reluctant to start with, but he searched his cupboard and gave her the details. Molly promised to put money into the account the next day and left.

Molly felt strange and embarrassed. She was drawn into uncharted waters by a man whom she had met recently. She could not confide in anybody or seek advice about how to deal with him if it happened again. Three weeks later, she got a text from Cliff asking whether she would like to meet up so that they could have a catch up.

Molly didn't know what to do. She felt trapped. Anyway, she decided to go and texted him accordingly.

One day, Mark phoned Jim to come over and wanted to talk to him. Jim was worried about his illness and whether he had developed any complications. Jim called in that afternoon.

As soon as he sat down, Mark said, 'I have only you to ask this favour. I need some money urgently. I wanted to get—'

'Look, you don't need to tell me any details of the why and wherefore of your need for the money. Just tell me how much?'

'£2,500; is that possible?'

'It is not just a possibility; it is a surety. Your need is my need. Your problem is my problem. Your headache is my headache.'

'I shall return it in six months. Is that OK?'

Jim just paused for a moment. 'Just leave it with me.'

Mark asked, 'Is it yes or no?'

'You should know that there is only one answer: **yes**.'

Jim left shortly afterwards. He went straight to the bank and arranged a transfer of £2,500 into Mark's account. He rang Mark the next day and told him that the money had gone into his account. Mark thanked him a lot.

Mark's condition was deteriorating steadily with the significant escalation of his care needs. Molly found it beyond her capacity to look after him at home. After a family discussion, Mark agreed to move into St Mary's Hospice. The hospice care aimed to improve the quality of life and well-being of adults and children with a life-limiting or terminal condition. It helped people live as fully and as well as they could to the end of their lives, however long that may be.

Jim used to visit Mark twice weekly and spend time chatting. He used to pop in usually late afternoons. Molly had a customary sleep after lunch. She started resenting Jim's visits. She started hating him, his ways, his visits and his whole persona. But she did not have the courage to stop him. Even if she did something to stop it by way of telling the hospice staff, she was scared that Jim would find out and the consequences would reflect badly on her.

Molly's thoughts started wandering. While reading the newspaper, there was a report on assisted dying. Although she did not know much about it, as usual, she had her opinion on everything. She felt there was no harm in 'helping somebody'. She went to the library and got books on dying. The Oxford Dictionary definition caught her eye - a gentle and easy death, the bringing about of this, especially in the case of incurable and painful disease. In 2003, Mr Reginald Crew, a 74-year-old man suffering from motor neurone disease and terminally ill, went to Switzerland 'to die with dignity.' His wife, who was beside him at the time of death, remarked, 'All he has done has been to go a tiny bit earlier. He was just choosing the right moment.'

After reading the books, she made the following notes and kept reading them again and again to digest and understand it better:

The Suicide Act 1961 decriminalised suicide and attempted suicide. Suicide is a person intentionally killing himself. But if a person refuses life-saving treatment because he wants to die, the argument is he is committing suicide by act of omission. On the other hand, if a person acts knowing that death will result, but not acting for the purpose of dying, it is committing suicide. The courts have not been clear in this regard. The Secretary of State for the Home Department v Robb [1995] Fam 127, Lord Justice Thorpe stated that a prisoner who went on hunger strike and as a result died, did not commit suicide.

Euthanasia: there are five countries where Euthanasia is practiced legally including our neighbours Belgium and Netherlands. Arguments for, are - (a) slow, painful, pain-filled death is horrific (b) the society acknowledges right to autonomy. So, one should be able to make the most important and intimate decision of his life and how to end it. Arguments against are - (a) most crucial principle is sanctity of life and allowing euthanasia is blatant violation of this (b) The assumption that some lives are not worth living and lead to a situation that vulnerable people can be easily manipulated into agreeing for euthanasia.

Physician-assisted suicide: This is the physician giving assistance to enable his patient to commit suicide. This can be by providing drugs in sufficient amount to commit suicide. A modern computer-assisted system by which patient can self-administer lethal drugs also has been devised. Beauchamp and Childress (2003) suggested that assisted suicide can be justified if the 9-point checklist is satisfactory.

Public opinion: The British Attitudes Survey (Park, 2007) found that 80% of those surveyed said that the law should definitely or probably allow a doctor to end someone's life at the person's request if he has an incurable and painful illness from which he will die. In 1994, The House of Lords Select Committee on Medical Ethics commented on public opinion on euthanasia- Polls are difficult to interpret and subtle changes in the wording of the questions can produce startlingly different results.

Hardwig (1997) argued – To think that my loved ones must bear whatever burdens my illness, debility or dying process might impose upon them is to reduce them to means to my well-being. That would be immoral. Baroness Warnock (2001) commented about those suffering from dementia – If you are demented, you are wasting people's lives, your family's lives and you are wasting the resources of the NHS. Daniel Callaghan suggested that once a person has reached a certain age, he has lived a 'fair innings' and extensive medical intervention to prolong his life should not take place. This is advocating non-intervention in later years.

One day, Jim dropped in about 3.30 in the afternoon. Mark was sat up in bed. He asked, 'Are you OK?' Mark greeted him with his customary smile which has his patent on it. As usual, he made enquiries about his well-being and sat down talking. Jim went to the loo. When he returned Mark said, 'Molly has nipped out to the corner shop; also she likes to go for a walk to get some fresh air.'

As Jim sat down, Mark leaned forward towards him, squeezed Jim's hand and said in an apologetic tone, 'You know Molly is diabetic. She also has a blood pressure problem. She has to take tablets at lunchtime and rest after that.'

Jim said, 'So, what do you want me to do?'

'The evening visiting time is six until eight. But, as you know, you are exempt from that. I already told the staff that you are part of the family and could visit any time.' Mark released the pressure of his squeezed hand, gave a deep sigh and gazed vacantly through the window.

Jim listened very carefully. Then he stayed still like a statue for a couple of minutes, blankly without any emotion or thoughts. Jim's voice quivered as he started talking.

'No problem; I will come during visiting hours.' He felt that although Mark had drawn him into the inner rhythm of his family knowingly, there were forces acting on gravely ill Mark to sever the rhythm.

A barn owl sat on the nearby acacia tree, hooted twice. The hoots of an owl frequently create a spooky and unnerving atmosphere. In many cultures, the appearance of owls is seen as a bad omen or a sign of death.

Jim had to go to Germany on a work-related matter urgently for two weeks. He had a hectic schedule. He phoned the hospice reception and requested to leave a message with Mark about his Germany trip and that he would be dropping in for a few minutes about 4.30 in the evening. As soon as Jim walked in, Molly left saying that she had to go the post office.

As Jim sat down, Mark asked him to pull the chair closer to him, held his right hand firmly almost squeezing and started talking.

'I heard you are off to Germany.'

'Yes, I am going tomorrow. I will be back in a couple of weeks.'

'I want to tell you some things. I have already talked to Molly, Julie and Jacob about all this that I am going to tell. When you came back, I may not be here.' Mark reflected in a serene and remote tone.

Jim said, 'It is not in our hands; the Lord decides and takes care of what is in store for us.'

Mark replied, 'When I go, you and you only have to give the

eulogy in the church. You must oversee whatever is needed. Since you are the only person who knows me in and out, you should write an obituary in the *Yorkshire Post*, since I have lived in Yorkshire most of my working life. You must visit my home as usual, once a fortnight. Although I will not be there physically, my spirit will be there. When you come, you must sit on my usual chair because you are my replacement in all family matters. Both Julie and Jacob are young. They do not have much worldly knowledge. You must look after them and give them the right advice, there is nobody wiser than you, in my knowledge. They are lucky to have somebody like you to go to. Also, if you need anything, don't hesitate to ask them.'

Jim held his tongue, listened carefully and patiently fully respecting Mark's emotional state and sentiments. That was an exchange between two intelligent men with mutual esteem, held in a serene and solemn setting.

12

Journey's End

Mark's condition rapidly deteriorated. It had a knock-on effect on Molly. Jacob and Julie were witnessing the tell-tale signs. Molly was getting irritable and moody at the most trivial things. The sleepless nights, round the clock attendance and increasing physical and care needs of Mark were taking its toll on her.

One night, she felt very rough. She had a gin and tonic once, twice, and thrice. She felt a bit easy and laid down. A random thought just flew in like an intruder into her head. I can't keep doing this; I'm worn out. Anyway, he is going to die; it is only a question of when. I have been a slave all my life. I need to get out. I also have a life. There must be a way out. This is the best chance. Jim will be away. He is highly intelligent. If he is around, he will smell a rat. It must be done soon. Come on Molly be brave and put your thoughts into action.'

Molly became restless in body and mind. She developed palpitations, flushing and her head was spinning. She went into the porch and gazed. She noted a sparrow in the garden struggling, dragging one leg; it was in agony and pain. In a flash, a palm-nut vulture whisked the hapless bird in flight; the suffering bird's life on earth ended abruptly.

The next day, Molly asked Jacob, 'Has Jim gone to Germany? Do you know when he will be back?'

'Yes, uncle will be back in 12 days. Why? Do you need anything?'

'No, just checking. Because Mark is going down, I am worried that Jim won't be around.'

Jacob replied, 'Let us hope uncle will be here.'

'Hope so, but don't bother to contact or trouble him. He might have gone on important matters.'

'Yes, Mum.'

'If we need to contact him, I will tell you.'

'OK.'

The dye was cast. Molly's thoughts ran amok. The man who knows all about Mark is out of the country, out of sight. Put out Mark; kick out Jim; get all the money; start a new life. She popped out to the corner shop, got gin, brandy and a few onions.

By 8.30 at night, Mark was given his usual tablets; he appeared very frail, coughed twice and slowly slipped into sleep.

Molly went into the porch and made her show-off piece of 'Harvard' cocktail - brandy, vermouth, Angostura bitter and sugar syrup. She had two sips; she couldn't stay still, started pacing up and down. She tried to focus on the job ahead. Nobody can, nobody will know what is going on in the room, she thought. All my friends know Mark is very poorly. Jim is out of the country. I will not get another golden chance like this.

The phone rang about 10.30pm. It was Julie ringing to say that she had to take her car for a service and wouldn't be around till two in the afternoon. This disturbed Mark's sleep.

Best chance!

Molly went to the night nurse, 'Mark is very restless and not sleeping.'

The nurse dropped in ten minutes later and gave Mark two tablets and an injection. In half an hour, Mark slipped into narcosis.

Molly locked the room. Her mind started wandering helter-skelter. 'What if the plan fails? Rubbish don't think like that.

After all, a hospice is for people to die.

All of a sudden, there was a red and silver flash of lightning followed by thunder. Then the heavens opened. The heavy barrage of the rain thumping on the windows, stimulated her to spring into action sooner than later. Even if a shell lands on the roof, nobody is going to hear it. The deafening noise went up in pitch. Is Mother Nature doing a death dance?

Seize the moment!

Oh, I am only trying to ease his burden, trying to help him on his way out. Stop the suffering! Let him go. I love him; do I or do I not?

The glass window vibrated with another bout of thunder and lightning.

Time to act!

Molly walked slowly, bare-footed, looked at Mark in the dim light, took a deep breath, paused, gave him a kiss on the forehead.

'Goodbye! I will join you later.'

She put the heavy bath towel over Mark's head, pressed hard may be for a minute. His right hand twitched twice symbolizing goodbye. The frail figure fainted and faded away. His last breath was held in suspended animation. The flame was extinguished.

That was it; job done.

Moly started pacing around.

Well, I have only cut short his suffering.

Her mind started playing games.

'Come on; calm down,' she said to herself.

She went into the porch. There was bottle of Chateau Pierron red wine sitting with an inviting critical grin at her. She poured it into the glass with a gurgle, looked at it and thought, is there blood in it? Oh, my God, Is there blood on my hands? Don't be silly.

She finished the glass in a hurry, burped twice and poured another round and took it down, lay on the settee and sipped slowly in bouts. She dosed off in spells.

Not poppy nor mandragora, Nor all the drowsy syrups of the world, Shall ever medicine thee to that sweet sleep which thou ow'dst yesterday - the words in Shakespeare's play *Othello*, rang in her ears.

Being a reader in the church, the reading from Romans 3:13 flashed in her head: Their throats are open graves; their tongues practice deceit. The venom of vipers is on their lips.

Am I one among them, she thought?

The chirping of birds came in bursts broadcasting from the surrounding treetops announcing the death of Mark, calling one another. It was half past five in the morning. The nurse usually came in at six to check.

She thought, let it look natural.

Molly looked at her hands. Words from Shakespeare's *Macbeth* started haunting her - All the perfumes of Arabia will not sweeten this little hand! Oh, oh, oh!

Oh, the evidence; I must destroy it. She looked at the bath towel. Is there blood on it? No, it is my imagination. Anyway, I must get rid of it.

She took the towel to the bathroom and urinated on it, not enough, defecated a bit, wrapped in a carrier bag, tied it up, labelled 'soiled - to dispose' and left it in the corner of the bathroom.

Molly took the latch off the door, so that the nurse could come in. I forgot something important, she thought. She went into the porch, wrapped the sliced onion and kept it in her handbag.

She laid on the settee, put the glass and bottle of wine on the table beside her and tried to compose herself. She went to the toilet and on the way back, had a quick glance at Mark. He was not breathing; she touched him. He had turned cold.

At ten past six, the nurse gave a gentle knock and breezed into the room. Molly lay on the settee with eyes closed, breathing heavily, feigning snoring.

The nurse checked on Mark. Oh, dear! Mark had passed away. She tried to wake Molly up.

Molly 'woke up' and turned towards the nurse with a sceptical lifting of the eyebrows and slurring of voice, 'What time is it?'

The nurse said, 'Ten past six. Sorry Molly, Mark has passed away in his sleep.'

'Oh, my God!'

Molly 'passed out' onto the settee.

The nurse came around, let her lie flat and comforted her. She asked, 'Shall I ring Jacob?'

Molly just nodded gently in approval. After the nurse had left, Molly used the onions to 'cry' and pulled up her chair and stayed leaning onto his body 'crying and sobbing.' She indulged in craven, self-preserving ritual actions.

Jacob and Julie arrived forty minutes later. Both started comforting Molly. Jacob went to the ward to discuss the formalities after death. Later in the day, the body was removed by the undertaker. Jacob rang close family friends.

The next evening, there was a meeting of eight people, close friends, to finalize the funeral arrangements. Neighbour, Edwin, enquired about the eulogy.

Molly butted in instantly. 'It should have been Jim. But he is away in Germany. So, I have arranged Francis,' (a neighbour but a total stranger to Mark and who Mark never liked), 'to do the job. She said it all in a single breath as if the speech was rehearsed. Jacob kept quiet.

Julie tried to rationalize with Molly. 'Uncle Jim is the most suitable and befitting person to say the eulogy. It is not impossible for him to come from Germany for a day or two.'

Molly abruptly interrupted, 'Well, there are a lot of things to sort out, especially bank accounts and sale of the property in Sri Lanka, which are for you both.' She was dangling the carrot to entice them to agree to her wishes. At that fatal moment, although she knew it was an aberration of Molly's judgement, Julie's mental resolve gave way and obliged Molly by agreeing with childish simplicity and vague thoughtlessness, when prudence and circumspection were warranted.

13

Farewell

Mark's body was kept at St James Funeral service. The funeral parlour was a swanky place, with its velvet drapes and upholstery, Queen Anne style furniture, polished glass tabletops and chandeliers. Molly made a solo trip to oversee matters. The staff noted a vacant masked look on her face.

The function was conducted as per the wishes of Molly. The hearse was a mahogany carriage with intricate carvings and black velvet drapes with glass sides so that by-passers could see the coffin. It was pulled by two black Schweres Sachsens horses. The journey was unique - after leaving the parlour, family accompanied the body in a black limousines. The group arrived at home, friends and relatives paid homage and then proceeded to the church following the hearse.

The funeral was at St Joseph's Church, which was of Gothic architecture, an architectural style in Europe that lasted from the mid-12th century to the 16th century, particularly a style of masonry building characterized by cavernous spaces with the expanse of walls broken up by overlaid tracery. The rib vault, flying buttress, and pointed arch were used as solutions to the problem of building a very tall structure while preserving as much natural light as possible. Stained-glass window panels rendered startling sun-dappled interior effects. One of the earliest buildings to combine these elements into a coherent style was the Abbey of Saint-Denis, Paris. Perpendicular style,

Phase of late Gothic architecture in England roughly parallel in time to the French Flamboyant style. The style, concerned with creating rich visual effects through decoration, was characterized by a predominance of vertical lines in stone window tracery, enlargement of windows to great proportions, and conversion of the interior stories into a single unified vertical expanse.

The six pallbearers appeared blinded and stifled under the black velvet clothing with golden borders, covering the coffin. Only the twelve legs were manifestly visible when the body was brought into the church.

The coffin was in dark-stained cherry with cushioned and quilted silky lining. It looked quite comfortable and inviting. The coffin gleamed in the light that streamed through the church windows. It was expertly crafted not only to bring comfort to the departed but also to smooth the living as well. It was built with love to be the final resting place of one who had been so adored in his lifetime. Its faux-gold handles and polished sheen were worth noting. There were flowers on the top that would be placed at the gravestone, everything beautiful to hide a reality of the hearts of the living kith and kin could not bear. Mark was brought there to be entrusted to God, to pray that he takes good care of him, as in their hearts they knew he would.

White lilies were laid on the coffin, traditionally symbolising sympathy, innocence, and a return to peace. Revered by the Greeks and the Romans and referenced in the New Testament and by Shakespeare, Lilies are renowned for their elegant beauty. There were some gladioli flowers. Named after the Latin 'Gladius' or sword, they were said to have been worn around the necks of gladiators to protect them from death. Their historic association with gladiators led gladioli to be used traditionally, as funeral flowers for men. More generally, they are used to represent strength of character and integrity There was a_standing sympathy spray to symbolize the way the departed filled hearts with love. Asymmetrically arranged with fresh white roses, lilies and carnations, green hydrangeas, this was a grand tribute to perfectly express the wishes for peace, serenity and hope.

But all at once heaven seemed so far away and they would be glad of this grave to visit when they needed him. Then too they would bring the flowers and imagine him safe and sleeping in this fine casket.

The church was full of friends, family and ex-work associates. It was well attended. An eight-year-old girl in the congregation asked her mum what cremation is.

She replied, 'When we burn the dead body of a person according to all the rituals that is known as cremation.'

The girl continued. 'Has uncle's spirit gone to heaven, or has he had to wait until his body was buried?'

The mum couldn't answer and kept quiet.

The service was being carried out by the priest. Watching the sequence of burial then leaving the funeral service and burial feeling broken up inside, asking Is this it?

During the service, a favourite song of your beloved, may be played, interspersed between eulogies and readings. If possible, I like to let the audience know that the song selected was important to the deceased and explain why. then it comes to funeral songs, the goal is to select ones that help the attendees reflect on and remember the life that was, and the passing of time.

As the guests arrived for the service, quiet background music was played to set the mood and allow attendees to quietly reflect on the life of the deceased. Molly kept on searching her handbag to get out the onions and keep on 'crying.'

Songs played at funerals are spiritual, celebrating one's belief of heaven, and life after death.

Music plays an important role and time should be spent choosing the best songs to play at a funeral. A loved one's death will be a hard time for you and your family. Not only do you have to cope with the loss of an important member of your family, you will also have to make the necessary preparations for a funeral or other memorial service. Getting the help of a funeral director is essential as he or she can help you in handling a lot of matters regarding the funeral and selection of songs. However, even though they may provide suggestions, it is really up to you to decide on what songs to play at the funeral.

The songs played were, 'My heart will go' on by Celine Dion and 'Yesterday' by The Beatles.

The eulogy was delivered by Francis, although Mark had specifically requested Jim to do it and had instructed Molly, Jacob, and Julie. This was an act of betrayal to Mark at his last hour on earth by own kith and kin. The oath of troth was blatantly breeched. Jim, the gentleman who had been Mark's life-long friend through his ups and downs, who lent dying Mark significant money and who helped him in so many ways, was forgotten and forsaken. When Francis went up to say the eulogy, there was a controlled whisper among the congregation asking the question, 'Why Francis? Where is Jim?.

Somebody remarked, 'Something is rotten in the streets of Denmark.'

Halfway through the service, Molly noted two policemen wandering through the car park. She had an apoplectic attack; threw her head back and collapsed due to intense fear of being arrested. Jacob, Julie, and others tried to revive her and in two minutes she came around. Shakespeare's words - They whose guilt within their bosom lies, imagine every eye beholds their blame. In fact, the passing policemen noted an uninsured vehicle in the car park, and they wanted to nail the party. They used their prudence to wait until the service was over to deal with the matter. Molly produced a smokescreen that being diabetic, her blood sugar dropped down since she did not feel like eating anything before the funeral. One lie led to another.

The service lasted an hour, the ceremony was conducted by Fr Thomas. The congregation left the church towards the funeral plot. During the short sojourn to the plot, Molly had a grapple in the grave. Being a minister of the church, she knew that Mark's death being unnatural in nature, was questionable in consecrated ground in front of the church. Conflicts and contrivances flooded into her heart. There was an influx of self-reproachful thoughts and feelings. However, she tried to find solace in the fact that the church receives the serf and the monarch on equal footing, just as they are in the sight of God. After all, all came from Adam and Eve.

At the burial site, pallbearers carried the coffin to the grave and placed it on wooden struts and positioned lowering straps through the handles of the coffin. When the command was given by the priest, the coffin was lifted by the straps, allowing the wooden struts to be removed, and then lowered into the grave. Mark was laid to rest and departed the world. As per Mark's wish, a wooden cross was erected facing the East (Orient), whence in the hope of resurrection, he would await the second coming of the Saviour.

Soon after the service, people started talking mainly about what happened to Jim. Molly had anticipated that and had already discussed with Jacob and Julie on the eve of the funeral to spread the news that Jim went to Germany although he knew Mark was gravely ill. This was a concerted ploy to subjugate Jim's image fomented by Molly to discredit Jim so that he would be tainted in infamy as a profile in cowardice. Like the Chernobyl nuclear accident, there was an incredible fall-out on the uneasy congregation. Most of them who knew the integrity of Jim, smelt a rat. Most in the congregation were in anticipation and speculation of a solemn and serene eulogy from Jim.

Many people who knew Jim thought that this was cruel, crash and caluminatory about him. A common friend, Matthew, rang Jim and told him about the funeral and eulogy.

Then Jim replied, 'Almost three hundred years back, Alexander Pope remarked - Fools rush in where angels fear to tread.' The news pulled on Jim's heartstrings. It was a full-frontal assault on his life-long friendship with Mark. Although it shook him, it did not affect his profile as a man of principle and courage.

After Mark's death, both Jacob and Julie felt very intimidated within the house. They were walking on eggshells tiptoeing most of the time. Molly acted with an aura of obfuscation, lackadaisicalness, and mystifying spin. She insisted her views to be intoned and not let them act like lackeys of deceased Mark. The tectonic differences in her agenda in contrast to those of Jacob and Julie, started causing gulfs in the unity of the family fabric. The rabble of visitors coming to see Molly were a mélange of riffraff, with whom she frolicked with fervour.

Jim went to Mark's house on return from Germany. He found the household was very cold-shouldered. Only Molly was in. The cleaner was tidying the rooms. Jacob and Julie had gone out. Molly's face was sombre, sulky and glazed like a blank sheet of paper. Being in a period of bereavement, Jim allowed some leverage. He passed on condolences and stayed mute much of the time.

Jim noted Molly was tensed up and clenching her hands together so that the knuckles appeared paler. As Jim sat down, her black eyes were blazing and glaring. She tossed back her mane of black hair extensions and her movements were brusque.

After going to loo when Jim returned to the living room, he noticed that the Glen Fiddich whisky on the table had vanished into thin air and a cheap Lambrusco wine has taken its place. Jim got the message loud and clear. He slumped onto the settee with his face dejected and brows creased. When Molly came with tea, he politely did not even take a sip saying that he had an upset tummy and had just been drinking bottled water only.

There was a dull, grey mass of gloom permeating in the air. A dark shadow fell upon the house. Unhappiness was written over the walls. Nothing could be spoken or asked. Jim felt like holding his breath. The clutch of discomfiture was stifling. Jim felt that his heart was scored and stabbed. Molly went to answer the phone in a hurry. Jim overheard some muttering of incoherent syllables which splashed out in the conversation.

A deep sense of silence and discomfort filled the room with suffocating stillness. Words got stuck in Jim's throat. He wanted to know a lot more about the funeral. But he chose not to ask. She conversed in sombre monologues. Looking out through the window, Jim noted the sky which was like molten gold. After exchanging banal enquiries about the well-being of Molly, Jim decided to leave. There was not a moment to lose. Molly put on the facade of a plastered smile. Masquerading her grief-struck demeanour, there was a whirlwind force of grotesque greed galvanizing her life.

Driving back, Jim could not fathom out what had happened to the house which Mark had told him many times 'was your own.' But he felt bereavement was a difficult and traumatic phase; so the best thing was to allow time and space and not to disturb them in any way.

Getting home, Jim tried to have a balanced view and thought

about how one of the bitter experiences in life is being betrayed. Betrayal is serious because it destroys trust, and without trust there can be no relationships. Without trust, society, families, institutions and most certainly a marriage cannot function. Betrayal shakes a person to his core because it ruptures his ability to trust. He tried to analyze what had gone wrong with Molly. The first was excessive ambition or greed. When a person cannot control or is overcome with these vices, she was liable to betray. It was greater than any sense of loyalty, integrity, or honesty she might have had in the past. A person's need to be wealthy and lead a luxurious life may cause her to steal, embezzle or misuse information given to her in confidence.

The second reason could be a feeling that betrayal is necessary to get greater achievements. Betrayal in this instance was not considered evil by the perpetrator. The third reason could be because people like to prove how smart they were. Many people like to play with others' minds, manipulate lives just to stir up trouble.

Betrayal was terrible because it caused Jim who has been betrayed to question his ability to trust again and it also caused him to question his own judgement. It partially destroyed his self-confidence.

Being an ardent Christian and scholar, Jim recollected: do not pay anyone back evil for evil, but focus your thoughts on what is right in the sight of all people. If possible, so far as it depends on you, live in peace with all people. Romans 12:14-19.

Two days later, Julie had a dentist appointment in the morning. Molly asked Jacob for a lift to go to the bank and casually asked him about how much was left to pay off his car loan. In fact, Molly had received the letter from Legal & General Insurance that the life insurance would pay out of £500,000 and will be put in her account. There was another £340,000 in various bank accounts, shares, and pensions.

Jacob went up, checked the file and told her that the outstanding balance was £18,700 and it was being paid monthly from Barclays Bank account. They reached the bank. Molly went into the bank saying,

'Can you stay in the car?' She returned after fifteen minutes and said she was very hungry, didn't have breakfast and asked Jacob to go to *La Vella* Italian Restaurant.

They sat down. The waitress came and took the drinks order. With a subtle smile and deep stare, Molly gave Jacob the bank credit slip showing she had paid off the car loan. Jacob nearly passed out with the sudden influx of a rainbow of emotions of joy, bliss and fortune.

He cried out in disbelief, 'I am the luckiest man on earth, to have such a wonderful mother-in-law.' She started snitching and snaking on his relationship with Julie.

Molly dreamed, the plan has worked; he is in my pocket. What more do I need to do to keep him on my side and guessing? I need to manipulate him more. She was deviant and mendacious.

'Well, it is only the start; you know all the money is for you and Julie only. What do you think? Should we sell the house in Sri Lanka? I think so; I want you to discuss with Julie and move forward.'

Jacob kept quiet.

She retorted, 'Did you hear me?'

'Yes, I did, Mummy. Mummy, by the by, has Uncle Jim's debt been paid off?' He enquired in a pensive mood.

She took umbrage at the question and trembled with apoplectic rage. Molly's features tightened; her dark face turned scarlet, and her eyes shot fire. 'Yes.' Molly shouted in an abrupt stern tone, then looked out through the window and said, 'It's going to rain; let us make a move.' Molly's guilt sat not only in her chest but also inside her brain. What she had done she could not un-do. She could make amends in subtle ways, but confession was out of the question to the priest. Only in her silent prayers could she speak her heart to God and beg for His mercy. She didn't feel like she deserved the love of Jesus Christ, but she clung to it and hung the shreds of her sanity on it. She prayed that one day she would feel removed from her sin, washed clean of it, but the guilt was a stain on her, an ugly scar. She had to believe in redemption and rebirth, she had to leave her deeds in the past and move on.

The guilt was ice in her guts. It could be a thirty-four degrees outside but still she felt frozen inside. Neither she could not melt it on her own nor could anybody else shift it at all. Guilt was that suffocating, heavy feeling in the chest. She was not being able to concentrate on the daily mundane tasks at hand because she knew she had done something drastically wrong. She felt that incessant throb in her heart, telling her she should apologize to God. It might or might not stop after the apology. She thought, will I ever be exculpated?

Guilt paired with shame. Shame told her that she was a bad person and that she did not deserve peace. It dug up the past and threw it in her face reminding her of all the times she failed. Guilt made her cry and wished she could have done without all these. The thoughts were of fear of discovery, anxiety, and impending judgement.

It was not always because someone has done something they know was wrong and could not take back, so guilt rises as a means of preventing future pain from similar actions.

As much as people are quick to say something was not our fault or we should not feel guilty, a reality of life is that we all screw up sometimes. We make mistakes and sometimes those mistakes have significant consequences. Sometimes we fail to do things we wish we had done or should have done. That may be as large as a grievous error in judgment or mistake that led to a death.

Molly could not get to sleep. She kept on making the sign of the cross repeatedly without her knowledge. She started drinking wine but that did not help. Then she tasted Disaronno and coke and liked the taste. She drank five to six shots every night. Still she could not get to sleep. She felt scared. Although felt partially drunk, she kept on waking up in the early hours of the morning startled and perspiring with nightmares. A few times she felt that she was in a prison cell for her crime, only to wake up and find that she was on her bed.

The figure of Mark on his deathbed haunted Molly day and night. Although she tried to blank it out, his ever-smiling face and his voice kept marching through her mind. At times she heard knocks on the door and on opening, there was a man wearing a hat like Mark appeared in a flash and within the blink of an eye vanished. The smell of his favourite Cerruti fragrance kept lingering in the air. While staring into space, she heard a bout of laughter mimicking that of Mark's when he had a few shots of whisky.

She started screaming at night and kept wetting her bed often with urine and sometimes with faeces as well. One day, her next-door neighbour Margaret heard her scream about 4.30 in the morning. She was scared that Molly was being burgled or assaulted. She did not feel safe to come out. So, she rang 999 and informed the police. The police soon called around. Molly was in a shaken state. Her eyes were sore and burning due to lack of sleep. The police found nothing suspicious and documented it as a nightmare in their diary and suggested that she get a night carer before leaving. She had no joy, companionship, or warmth. She was flooded with guilt and fear which started eroding her. Later, Margaret called around and Molly offered tea. While chatting, she admitted that she was scared to sleep alone at night. Margaret felt pity on her seeing her gaunt look and sorrowful and bruised eyes. She was a tormented soul. When she went out, she dressed in an expensive saree and exquisite ornaments, cramming her inner struggles in mummery.

Two days later, the gardener phoned to say that he would not be able to work for six to eight weeks since he was going in for a back operation. But he would send a young man whom he knows, to tidy the garden temporarily. Molly agreed. The man came he next day and introduced himself as Gary, who was 23 years old, and the son of a property developer. He was doing a degree in Health and Social Care. He liked gardening which earned him decent pocket money. He was 5 feet 10 inches tall, with an athletic build, long brown hair tied into a bun, a thin beard, blue eyes and curly eyebrows.

Molly made a cup of tea and went up to Gary. He was bent down and pulling the weeds out. The sweaty ass crack was quite visible which triggered a wave of excitement in Molly. She admired his figure and youth and felt an irresistible desire to make friends with him. After he had left, Molly enquired further details from Margaret about Gary. He was from a rich family and of good background.

The next day, Molly rang him to thank him and started chatting. He said he does counselling also. Molly asked whether he could pop in for tea the next day. He agreed. Next day, Gary dropped in. Molly invited him to have tea and biscuits on the dining table. They started chatting. Molly explained her sleep problems and difficulties and scariness at night. He took pity on her. She asked whether he would consider a sleepover if needed.

He was agreeable. Gary started sleeping downstairs on the settee. He would come about 10 at night and leave by 6 in the morning. Two weeks later, Molly slipped in the bath and sprained her back. She was taking bed rest. When Gary came, he went up to see her. Molly asked whether he could give her a back massage. Gary obliged. He gave her a massage for half an hour; she felt a bit easier.

Two weeks later, it was Gary's birthday. Molly invited him for a drink and surprised him with a gift, a Ralph Lauren Polo Blue eau de toilette gift set. Gary was gobsmacked. Molly asked him to try it on. The fragrance was fresh and daring, presented in a luxurious, plastic-free gift box, the set contained a 125ml eau de toilette and a 30ml plus a Ralph Lauren travel pouch featuring the iconic Ralph Lauren polo pony. In Polo Blue Eau de Toilette, Ralph Lauren has bottled the freedom of the blue sky, the energy of the open waters and the warmth of the sun on your back, in one unique fragrance. The initial impression of this fragrance is lush, masculine, and energizing, with melon and cucumber bringing an invigorating burst of freshness. Aromatic heart notes of Sage, Geranium, and Basil create a natural, aromatic sensuality. Finally, the warm and enveloping base notes of Suede, Patchouli, and Sheer Musk leave long lasting and unique trail. Molly ordered a five course Sri-Lankan meal from the take-away and they enjoyed the night. She tittered coquettishly with Gary about so many trivial things.

About six weeks after Mark's death, Jacob rang Jim and enquired whether he had any telephone messages from Mark saved on his phone. Jim thought it was a strange enquiry especially since that was the only time Jacob spoke to him after Mark's death. When he enquired why, Jacob replied in a subdued and muffled way,

'Mummy wanted to listen to retrieved messages of Dad to

make an album.'

Jim said there were no messages. In fact, it was Molly's ploy to find out if there were any clues implicating her. Jim thought, suspicion always haunts the guilty mind.

14

Parted Ways

The vast amount of money changed and transformed Molly into somebody else; someone who started spending money profligately and prodigiously in a fiercely reckless manner. The abundant richness propelled her higher up in the social circle. Money makes the world go round.

Life had a new radiance and different direction, an unchartered buoying corridor of journey. Molly started weaving daydreams. Her dream of a lifetime was coming true after accruing lots of money and properties as her own. She felt that she was like a bank of some proportion rather than a private person, due to the euphoric effects of solvency and freedom to act without any curbs.

Gary did not have a passport. Molly went to the post office and got an application form. She persuaded Gary to apply and paid for it. Once Gary got it, he informed Molly. She started spending money extravagantly, buying expensive sarees, enjoying frequent weekend trips with Gary to Paris, Amsterdam and Frankfurt. Gary felt that she was profligate in her manners, but he went along with her wishes since he had never tasted any luxury in his life. She led an improvident lifestyle. In the household, she promoted herself as the matriarch. An aura of repression and regression set in. To stay in overall control, she also orchestrated cat and mouse game between Jacob and Julie, which led to more sinister game of snakes and ladders as time went on. Mark's death anniversary was conducted. About seventy-five people - family and friends - were invited. Jim was totally ignored. A week later Jim rang Jacob casually wanting to speak to him. He said he was 'busy' preparing a court case. He never bothered to return the telephone call.

Jim was invited to Maxine's wedding (a common family friend's daughter). He sent an RSVP saying that he would be attending. Molly rang Maxine's mother Edith to find out the table arrangements at the reception dinner and who else was invited. Two days later Molly felt irritable, started pacing up and down and rang Edith back to change sitting arrangements and sit with three other friends away from Jim's table.

Jacob was promoted to barrister. Again, Jim was never informed. He held a celebration party in the church hall. Later a grand party was held at Hotel Imperial for forty-five VIP couples.

Molly coaxed Jacob to get a Maserati Quattroporte car after trading in the Volvo. She paid off the difference. The first week after getting the car, she arranged for Fr Thomas to bless the car on a Sunday morning before mass. Afterwards, she made it a habit to ensure that she came 15 minutes early for the Sunday mass to enable parking near the entrance of the church so that all the worshippers could see the glamourous car. After the service, she also used to wait to lean on the car and chat with all coming out after the service. She made a spectacle of herself, and these repeated episodes got her the nickname 'Hyacinth' from the TV show, *Keeping up Appearances*. People started avoiding her by leaving the service a few minutes before finishing time. At Easter time, she contributed to the local charity of disabled children. She attitudinized the situation and the photograph of her presenting the cheque to the secretary was published in the local newspaper with the newly acquired car in the background.

Molly started going on weekend trips with friends. She said it was with National Holidays and would get a taxi to the pickup point. One day while shopping in ASDA, Julie caught up with a neighbour, Janet. Janet invited her for a coffee. While chatting she described her coach trip to Llandudno, a coastal town in North Wales. It is known for North Shore Beach and 19th-century Llandudno Pier, with shops and a games arcade. Northwest of town, the cliffs of Great Orme headland jut into the sea. Ancient tunnels lead to a cavern at Great Orme Mines. A 1902 tramway has an upper and lower section, and travels to the headland's summit. To the east, smaller headland Little Orme is a nature reserve. She described the trip in detail and casually mentioned that Molly was on the trip with a young guy. From the description, Julie knew it was Gary. She didn't bother about Molly's newly found freedom, love and enthusiasm. Molly's mind had mysteriously and monotonously turned into a minefield of self-interest and promotion of her ego. She deliberately distanced herself from Jacob and Julie and avoided discussion of matters of common household interest. Molly's mysterious movements caused worms of doubt in the heads of Jacob and Julie.

Charlotte's birthday was approaching. Jacob started feeling uneasy and restless contemplating what to do. Jacob mentioned to Julie that he was planning to go to London the next weekend for a two-day conference. Julie did not ask him the details.

Jacob rang Charlotte and said, 'I am planning a mystery weekend together next week; can we leave Friday evening and come back Sunday evening?'

Charlotte kept mute for a few seconds out of sheer surprise.

Jacob reminded that it was the birthday treat.

She then murmured ,'Ok, if you wish so.'

They caught the *Pride of Rotterdam* ship from Hull at seven in the evening to Rotterdam, on a twelve-hour sailing. Jacob gave an overall description of the ship. The ship was christened by Queen Beatrix of the Netherlands and set sail for the first time in 2001. With several bars, restaurants, casino, shops, cinema and a show lounge spread across her 12 decks, she also has 546 cabins, 1360 passengers and has a lane capacity of 3,300 metres with space for 250 cars and 400 freight vehicles.

Though she was outwardly affectionate, considerate, and charming, he noticed a curious lack of warmth on Charlotte's part. It didn't take long for her to admit that she was about to come on her monthly soon. They went to the brasserie and chose a table overlooking the sea and ordered a bottle of Louis Roederer Cristal champagne.

Jacob was wearing a white full sleeve shirt and black trousers. The mustard moleskin waistcoat matched the bright gold bowtie. His gold-plated Jean Pierre Classic Tourbillon cufflinks were sparkling in the diffused light as he moved around. Charlotte wore a pink floral Ted Baker midi dress.

Jacob gave Charlotte total freedom to choose from the menu. While she was going through the menu, Jacob's eyes were scanning the multitude of diners flowing into the restaurant. For her starter, she chose Lentil soup. The soup was delicious. When Jacob enquired about the choice, she remarked with a grin,

'The name is derived from famous Roman family Lentulus. In Latin, *Lentus* means slow. It is thought that the moisture in lentils induced heaviness of mind and made men more reserved.' The main course composed of sweet and sour pork, halibut in piquant sauce well-decorated with cherry tomatoes, sweet pepper, and coriander leaves. There were gratin potatoes and Waldorf salad to go with. The dessert was Pavlova cake topped with whipped cream and decorated with fresh raspberries. Jacob could not resist an additional helping of chocolate cake. Then they had coffee to wind down. After the dinner, they strolled around the deck.

They noted two small passerine birds. Being a bird-lover, Julie gave a vivid description.

'Their name came from the Dutch word mannekijn, meaning little man. The stubby birds had short tails, rounded wings, and short bills with a wide gap. The females have dulled green colour and males hold black with striking patches. They are unique with many features, and among them, their voice box is a distinctive one. These romantic birds are blessed with beautiful sounds like whistles, trills, and buzzes. A further fantastic feature of these birds is the unique mating dance. The long-tailed males know the importance of a partner in their life. About seven years a master bird and a female bird will practice dance. They will practice to give a better dance in front of the female bird. They will perform it in a super way and with better synchronization. At the end of the performance, the female will choose a pair to have romance. The master of the team always gets selected for this, and then they love each other. The entire process of dance and the selection is a beautiful scene for the eyes. The little birds also shower flowers of romance with their unbeatable dance. They thus acquire the place in most romantic animals all over the world.'

After twenty minutes they reached a bar where many people were dancing. The uncontrollable desire to rub her assets onto Jacob's body overtook her mind. Although he was not the tallest or most handsome in the room, she felt he was like a superstar.

Charlotte pulled Jacob towards her, embraced her and said, 'I am kidnapping you and taking you by force to dance with me.' Jacob kept mute staring into her eyes in anticipation. They joined a group who were in a waltz. Her warm breath breezed against Jacob's neck insinuating every pore and invigorating every sinew. The soft and curvy breasts rubbed against the rock-hard chest of Jacob, the friction producing megawatt energy. Every part of their bodies was zinging with intense desire to immerse into one another. It was subtly romantic dance feeling slow and graceful. They moved across the floor in each other's arms in sway, rise and fall. There was five minutes break. After that, the DJ announced that the next item would be rumba. Charlotte swayed with Jacob close together with slow and sensual hip and leg movements.

They returned to the bar. Charlotte told Jacob to get whatever drink he liked and rushed to the toilet. Jacob got two cocktails. While she returned in haste, her pink cheeks were shining through and the eyes were emitting passion and lust. When she asked the name of the drink, Jacob kept smiling and said,

'I will leave it in suspense and tell you later. This has something to do with my job ahead tonight.' The drink was composed of grenadine, egg yolk, grenadine, and curacao.

In a few minutes, they returned to the cabin. Jacob sat on the bed and got the receipt from his pocket and thrust into her hands. It read '*2 x Bosom Caresser Cocktail.*' She burst into a bout of chilling laughter. She lowered herself onto his lap, sat on the throne and hugging him, deeply kissed him. Her tumbled hair was all over and got into Jacob's mouth. He gently pushed it towards the back of her shoulders and pulled her towards him. She got the intoxicating smell of brandy and fragrance in his breath. She gently went harder and thrust her tongue deep inside his mouth. He felt that a snake was restlessly probing the cavity of his mouth. When her tongue got rolled up and firm, it was like a deep-sea diver exploring the unfathomed cave of the ocean bed. In a few minutes she gently pushed him down onto the bed. They had a wonderful time.

In the morning, they got ready and went by coach to the city centre. After breakfast at a café, they started loitering along the shopping arcade. Jacob asked her to wait outside a shop and came back in a few minutes. He bought her a birthday gift, Black Opium perfume by Yves Saint Laurent. She was thrilled since it was her favourite.

They went back to the ship by teatime. It set sail at 6.30 as the return trip to Hull. They had dinner and went to the cabin early. The next morning by seven, the ship arrived at Hull Port. Jacob gave a lift to Charlotte and returned home.

The cleaners noted a lot of blood on the bed sheets in the cabin. They reported to the security staff suspecting whether there was any crime committed.

A week later, a letter arrived in a window envelope from P&O Ferries. When Julie checked the name of the addressee was not visible. She thought it was junk mail but decided to open before discarding. It was a shock to her system. The letter read that there was a significant amount of blood on the bedspreads in the cabin, which needed deep cleaning. Also, it was pointed out that Jacob was duty bound to report any unforeseen accident to them before disembarking. They needed a statement of what happened in the cabin.

Julie was deeply upset, angry and started pacing up and down. Then she drank two glasses of wine to calm down. She sat on the settee and got lost in thoughts contemplating how to handle this matter. She concluded that Jacob had been having an ongoing affair with Charlotte. Her anger slowly mellowed. She took a photocopy of the letter and stuck it back in the envelope, poured some water on it to make it look like the rain had damaged the envelope. She left it on Jacob's desk with other letters.

Julie wanted to find out more. She rang and talked to a private detective and got an appointment to see him. Later in the week, Julie went to the detective and briefed him on the situation. He collected Jacob's car number, job details etc and said he would monitor his movements and update her weekly. Julie started feeling low, lonely and lethargic. That evening she went to bed early. When Jacob returned by seven in the evening, she said she had a headache and didn't want to be disturbed.

Jacob casually went through the letters and when he read the P&O Ferries letter, his nervous system went into a state of shock. He envisaged the various ramifications and the potential aftermath which would wreck his marriage. He presumed that Julie had not seen the contents and pretended to be as normal as possible although his stomach was performing cartwheels.

Later, he showed the letter to Charlotte and carefully drafted a letter apologising for the mishap and that his wife had heavy and irregular periods. He gave his e-mail and requested them to correspond by e-mail if there were any further issues. A week later, he got an e-mail to state that they have accepted his apology and the matter has been settled without any further action. Both had a sigh of relief.

Both Jacob and Charlotte started feeling low and guilty. They kept seeing each other weekly and both were drinking too much. Jacob felt that he needed to show more love and care to her for her co-operation and consideration. The meetings turned out slowly to be more of drinking sessions. The private detective was keeping close eye of his encounters and fed Julie with all the details.

A few weeks later, Jacob phoned that he would be late returning home since he had a meeting. Julie informed the detective to monitor. Jacob was with Charlotte for over three hours. They both were drinking. Jacob got plastered and unsteady. He rashly took the car and drove home. It was quarter to eleven at night. Through the village in a 30mph zone, he was driving at 50mph. The police patrol car waiting near the pub noticed it and decided to chase him. He was stopped and charged with speeding and drink-driving. He had to abandon the car and get a taxi. When he got home, Julie had been pacing up and down. On opening the door, the strong smell of alcohol breezed through the gentle wind. Julie was incensed. Like a lioness stalking, she instantly pounced at the prey.

She screamed, 'Where have you been drinking? You have been with that whore! Off you go.' She pushed Jacob out and slammed the door. Instantly he felt hapless, helpless, and hopeless. Jacob just paused a couple of minutes and decided it was not the right time and place to engage in any conversation to give an excuse. He walked 200 yards, got out of Julie's sight, and rang for a taxi. He had nowhere to go but to Charlotte's flat.

When Charlotte opened the door, she knew that something catastrophic had happened. Jacob could not hardly speak. He looked miserable and weepy. She did not want to upset him further by talking. She held him and walked towards the bed, loosened his clothes, and asked him to sleep it off. Within a few minutes, Jacob went into deep slumber. She went to sleep hugging him.

***

Julie had lost her composure. She was shaking with rage, bitterness, and revenge. She had to tell Molly everything since after all a mother's advice would be the best she could get. Listening to Julie, Molly almost collapsed and sank onto the settee. She knew that her daughter needed prompt help and support to tackle this complex, concealed and convoluted situation. Although she patiently listened and nodded in approval to Julie, she recalled in her mind the extramarital affairs behind the back of Mark while she was away on her own. She pacified Julie and promised to help her out.

Jacob's troubles compounded. The drink-driving episode was not taken lightly by the partners in the law firm, although the senior partner was more sympathetic and understanding since he also was caught for the same offence ten years back. But the gossip about the affair with Charlotte spread like wildfire, like the hum of bees swarming in summer.

As the days and weeks went past, Jacob felt more and more isolated. Charlotte sensed it. Her feelings of compassion and care led her to invite Jacob to stay with her to give him warmth, love, and support. She reassured him that everything would be discrete and secret. Reluctantly Jacob agreed and moved into her flat. The romantic couple slowly transformed from flat mates into sleeping partners.

Four months later, Charlotte said that she did a pregnancy test and it was positive. Jacob had a shock. Both discussed the matter at length. Jacob was keen for a termination, but Charlotte wanted a few days to think it over. That kept him on tenterhooks. Five days later, she agreed to have the pregnancy terminated and went to the doctor to arrange it. Jacob gave a big sigh of relief.

Molly caught up with Jacob. They agreed to meet at a local restaurant to have a private discussion. She decided to talk to Jacob to get his side of the story. But Julie did not want him around her. It was a tricky situation. Jacob had to stay in a local bed and breakfast during that time. Molly went to see him to get to grips with the situation. Jacob sat poker-faced with an expression of condescending respect for his elderly mother-in-law and was not forthcoming with many details. To start with

Molly told him in confidence that Julie had unmistakable evidence from the detective of his unsavoury liaison with Charlotte. That threw him on the back foot.

The weight of his guilt hung over his neck like a hangman's noose. He sat speaking mechanically in a monotonous tone due to the innate anxiety boiling inside him. His countenance was riddled with sorrow and remorse. The fog of gloominess was in the air. He dug down and got some far-fetched mental reserve to search for any way out and lacked the onus of giving a clear and genuine explanation of the concatenation of events.

Molly suggested that the best option was for Jacob to stay separated for the time being until an amicable solution could be reached. After a lengthy chat, the agreed plan was that Jacob would stay separated for a short time until Molly could persuade Julie to be more accommodative, understanding, and willing to forgive and forget his misdemeanours. Julie was in no mood to forgive and stayed belligerent in her attitude to Jacob. Molly pleaded with Julie for an interim break and reassess the situation in four weeks.

Meanwhile the private detective had been monitoring Jacob. He was discretely videoing Jacob's movements and showed Julie the evidence. She went crazy and decided to see a solicitor with a view for divorce. Armed with the evidence, she saw the solicitor. She was advised that the divorce could be straight forward since the *res ipsa loquitor* (let fact speak for itself) principle would be applicable.

After lengthy discussion with the solicitor, Julie decided to stay officially separated. The solicitor wrote to Jacob. He had already thought along similar lines. He moved in with Charlotte. Molly spent time with different friends as and when it suited her aspirations and wishes, and she squandered lot of money.

Julie got unmistakable evidence from the private detective

that Jacob and Charlotte were co-habiting. She paused and pondered for a while before taking the final decision to go ahead with divorce. Thus, the young lawyer from Sri Lanka who migrated to the Land of Hope and Glory, turned out in hoop and gloom, losing the prime possession - the family. He ended up in the boulevard of broken dreams.

Life is fired at us at point blank range; one does not get the chance to do a rehearsal. Life is like a river. The way of life is to flow with the current. To turn against it takes effort, but the current will carry you if you let it.

Printed in Great Britain
by Amazon